HAUNT

To the Class of '88, Penketh High School, Warrington

HAUNT
DEAD
SCARED

CURTIS JOBLING

SIMON AND SCHUSTER

First published in Great Britain in 2014 by Simon and Schuster UK Ltd
A CBS COMPANY

1 3 5 7 9 10 8 6 4 2

Simon & Schuster UK Ltd
1st Floor,
222 Gray's Inn Road
London WC1X 8HB

Simon & Schuster Australia, Sydney
Simon & Schuster India, New Delhi

A CIP catalogue record for this book
is available from the British Library.

PB ISBN 978-1-47111-577-6
Ebook ISBN 978-1-47111-578-3

Printed and bound by CPI Group (UK) Ltd, Croydon, CR0 4YY

www.simonandschuster.co.uk
www.simonandschuster.com.au

ONE

First and Last

They say everyone has their soul mate. I found mine in pre-school. Actually, mine found me would be closer to the truth. I didn't want to be there – who would? I'd been ripped away from my mother's comforting embrace and forced into a realm of random toddlers and tantrums. Admittedly, on this occasion, I was the toddler having the tantrum, having been abandoned by Mum, but that's beside the point.

One inmate chose to take pity on me. It could have been the injustice of my plight that had drawn him to me. Perhaps my righteous bawling had struck a chord of brotherly love with him. I discovered years later he had his eye on my swanky new Ben 10 toy, but I won't quibble. I don't want to cheapen the moment. A quick hug, back pat and exchange of an action figure later, and our friendship was sealed. That was

1

a big day for me and Dougie Hancock: we've been best mates ever since.

Twelve years later, heading for Dougie's house, I was aware that I had a stupid grin plastered over my face. It had been there for the last ten minutes. I laughed out loud as I ped-alled, letting loose a brief *woo-hoo* that Homer Simpson would've been proud of. It had just gone nine o'clock, and St Mary's church bells were tolling nearby. I was going to be late getting in. Dad would probably have something to say about that, especially on a school night, but I didn't care. I had to get to Dougie's house, my good news couldn't wait. Not that he'd believe me, of course. I already knew he'd call me a liar, accuse me of having Munchausen's Syndrome. He might even say I was suffering from a head trauma, but still, I couldn't keep it to myself. I pedalled a little harder, my bicycle cutting up puddles and leaving spray in its wake.

Week nights I tended to stay in – except on Thursdays, when I went round to Dougie's to play Dungeons and Dragons and listen to his old indie albums. It's probably worth mentioning now that I was a bit of a geek, something the more mentally and emotionally challenged in school con-stantly mocked. They didn't like that my friends and I enjoyed roleplaying games as a hobby, didn't have girlfriends, or the fact that we read books and were able to string sentences together. Our ability to walk upright with little difficulty no doubt really put their noses out of joint too. It helped that Dougie was an even bigger nerd than me. The two of us drew strength from this bond, this brotherhood of geekdom. People could call my mates and I whatever names they wanted, we let it roll off us like water from a kaiju's back. Dougie and I were 'best mates through thick and thin'. I was the thin one … you can guess the rest. He was a kindred spirit to me, the Yin to my Yang, the Ant to my Dec.

Anyway, this chill November evening had been one that I would never forget. I'd spent it at the Square, the local precinct which was a hangout for many of the kids from school. In short, it's an intimidating place for a lad like me. I'm shy and a bit of an outsider, often looking in on the social gatherings of my peers like they're speaking another language. I wouldn't ordinarily have been there, but somehow I'd plucked up my courage and gone along. Something had happened that had turned my world upside down. It had been unexpected, it had been beautiful, and it had blown my tiny mind. We're talking Death Star explosion here. There really was only one person I needed to spill my gossip to, and I was fast approaching his house. I laughed out loud once more, giddy with my news and good fortune, imagining Dougie's face when I told him. I passed the road that I would ordinarily have turned off down, the one that led to my home. I didn't live far from Dougie – St Mary's graveyard and the school playing fields were all that separated our houses. I grinned to myself as I cycled the remainder of the journey to Casa Hancock.

It looked like an exciting new chapter in my life was just about to begin. Then again, fate can be a fickle beast.

I never saw the vehicle that hit me. I was doing everything right: staying close to the kerb, my lights on, both hands gripping the handlebars and brakes. It came out of nowhere. I heard the headlight shatter. I felt my bicycle crumple against the bumper as I flew out of the saddle, hitting the bonnet with a bang. My body spun as the car sped on, impacting with the windscreen before rolling like a ragdoll over the roof. Then the vehicle was gone and my broken body was flying through the air.

I was dead before I hit the tarmac.

TWO

Hit and Run

I never could stand hospitals. I'd been into Warrington General a couple of times for operations and neither of them had been pleasant experiences. Worst of all was last year's broken arm. I'd been playing football with my mates at lunchtime. It was only supposed to be a kickabout, a bit of fun. That hadn't stopped Milton, our Peruvian exchange student who was built like a brick outhouse, from charging into me and sweeping my legs clean out from under me. I quickly discovered they take their football very seriously in Peru. I flew up into the air and came back down to earth head first. Instinctively I put my left arm out to prevent myself breaking my neck, and my arm crumpled under my entire body weight. I was told later that the kids on the lower school playground had heard the *crack* a hundred metres away. When I got up I was holding my arm just below the elbow, revealing a perfect break halfway down my forearm. It was like an extra joint, the bottom portion swinging from an additional elbow. Two of my mates threw up at the sight and a nearby Year Seven girl fainted.

The nurse who'd seen me at the General Hospital had said it was just bruised. Admittedly my knowledge of medicine was limited but even I knew an additional pivot point in my forearm meant there was something very wrong.

Now here we were again. My parents sat on a bench in the corridor of the hospital, Mum staring off into space, her jaw slack. In her hands she clutched my scarf, the one she'd knitted, bound about her knuckles. I crouched in front of her, trying to catch her gaze, but she looked straight through me.

'Mum?'

Nothing, no response. She seemed calm but her unblinking eyes were screaming. Dad, to my surprise, was crying. I'd only seen him cry once before, when I was five years old and my grandpa passed away. He wept freely now, his arm around Mum.

'What's the matter?' I asked, but again was ignored.

My older brother, Ben, sat opposite them, eyes wandering over the linoleum floor. He was in sixth form and a tough act to follow. Straight As throughout his school career. Every teacher I ever met would greet me with the same phrase: 'Ah, another Underwood boy: I bet he's a prodigy just like his wonderful, frighteningly intelligent brother!' I had to work my backside off throughout school, just to follow in Ben's mighty footsteps. Talking of which, his foot now tapped out a beat on the floor, iPod headphones tucked into his ears. I sat down beside him, leaning in close. Unable to catch the tune, I reached for an earphone, ready to tug it out of Ben's lughole. I readied myself for the brotherly punch. That's what we did: I pulled out his earplugs and he gave me a dead arm.

But this time my fingers wouldn't connect with the little speaker on the wire. They went through the thin white cable, again and again, as I feverishly tried to grasp it. The headphones were passing *through* my fingers; no resistance, no sensation. Ben wafted his hand beside his head suddenly, as if batting away a fly. As if he didn't know I was there ...

'Ben!' I said, loud now. His foot kept tapping and his head remained bowed. I pulled away, looking down at my hands with incomprehension. They were so pale, almost translucent, a faint blue glow humming beneath the skin. I waved them before me, turning them over again and again. They left a blur before my eyes, as if moving in slow motion. This wasn't good at all. My stomach began to heave and lurch, a wave of dizziness crashing over me. I stumbled away from my family down the corridor, gasping for air, reaching out for the wall as I went.

My fingers passed through it, and my feet slipped through the floor as I struggled to keep hold of both my surroundings and my sanity. A doorway opened at the end of the corridor, dazzling bright white spilling into the passageway. Warm, white light. Welcoming. I felt an urge to see what was beyond the door, to pass through into the room beyond. My feet were no longer connected with the linoleum floor, my body blending with the world around me. All it would take was the will to move on, a nod of the head and I'd be through the doorway.

I turned to my left, my attention suddenly drawn away from the white room. It was another opening, close to where my folks sat, and utterly unremarkable compared to the glowing portal at the corridor's end. What caught my eye was a pair of scuffed trainers lying abandoned on a metal trolley. I knew that the white doorway wouldn't be open for ever, I was aware that I needed to get down there, and quickly, but I couldn't resist looking into this little side room off the corridor. Because the trainers were mine.

Leaving the glowing portal behind me, I allowed myself to be drawn into the room. As I entered I could feel my feet hitting the ground once more, each step away from the white light allowing me to reconnect with the world. It was an emergency room, another set of double doors exiting back into the Casualty ward. A body lay on a trolley, a white sheet covering it, an array of electronic equipment surrounding it. The 'pingy' monitors you see on the telly were there, but they were decidedly pingless. Another trolley held a grisly collection of bloodied tools – scalpels, forceps and freaky things that belonged in a horror movie. One of the trainers had been torn almost in half, while the other lay chopped up beside it. I'd saved up for ages to buy those trainers, and now some muppet had apparently taken a chainsaw to them. I bent down to look on the tray beneath – the rest of my clothes lay there, in an identical state of disrepair. Seriously, who had helped me out of these – Edward Scissorhands?

I looked down at my feet. There were my trainers, staring up at me: scuffed, battered, but in one piece. The same pale blue glow that ran through my hands emanated from them, running up my legs through my intact trousers and the rest of my body. My eyes drifted over the figure on the trolley. I moved further into the room to get a better look, the white light in the corridor dimming behind me.

There was no hiding from it. The truth was there as plain as the nose on my lifeless face. I looked down at my body, laid out on the bed. My skin was pale, the colour drained from it, and my lips had already taken on a blue hue, different to the glow that currently shone from my flesh. These lips were cold and bloodless. The left side of my temple looked depressed, as if it had been hit by a heavy object. The hair was matted with blood and gravel. Gravel from the road.

I reached a pale hand out tentatively, allowing my fingertips to brush my still face. No connection, no sensation. I recoiled, the full ramifications of my situation dawning on me. I made for the corridor again, quickly now, my cold corpse abandoned. Mum, Dad and Ben sat there in silence still, parents hugging, brother's foot tapping, each in their own broken world. I looked back down the corridor, knowing that I needed to go into the light now.

But the doorway was closing, the visible glimmer narrowing all the time. I hurried towards it, willing myself to fly as before, but my feet were too connected to the world of the living now. I stumbled and staggered, hands reaching out before me as I surged towards the light. Ten centimetres, five centimetres ... the gap of light was closing. Orderlies and doctors walked past, chatting and laughing. I ran through them, through any obstacle, as I sprinted towards the fading glow.

Two centimetres.

One centimetre.

The light blinked out and the doorway disappeared, replaced by a featureless magnolia wall. I hit the wall and passed right through it, out into the night beyond. Ambulances hurried by, lights flashing and sirens wailing as they went about their business. The illuminated exit was gone, replaced by the stars that shone down in the black night sky.

I looked at my hands once more. Pale blue. Ethereal. *Spectral*. My predicament was all too clear.

I was a ghost.

THREE

Sanderson and Sons

I'd never owned a suit, and never wanted to. It took my dying to get me into one. My wardrobe was full of jeans and indie T-shirts, which I suppose was hardly appropriate attire for the great hereafter. Mum and Dad fitted me up in a nice black suit instead. I looked like a gangster, laid out in my coffin – albeit a pretty small one with floppy hair and a smattering of zits. You could hardly see them, to be fair – the make-up artist in the funeral home had done a decent job. I thought I'd never be seen dead wearing make-up. Turns out that was wrong.

Sanderson and Sons was the oldest funeral home in Warrington and had taken care of my grandparents before me, so the place wasn't entirely alien, though my memory of running about the venue as a five-year-old was quite hazy.

Ben and I had been gathered in a back room with my cousins, where we'd played with our Action Men. It was a bit like a Christmas family get-together, although everyone was miserable. Actually, it was *entirely* like a Christmas family get-together.

Those cousins who I'd played with ten years ago were here now, dressed in black and suitably sombre. Mum, Dad and Ben were sat in the front pews, my extended family surrounding them. Ben was holding up well. He was tough, always had been. He might have only been two years older than me, but emotionally he was twenty years senior. Teachers always mentioned how he had his 'head screwed on straight', which is pretty handy, anatomically speaking. He'd help Mum and Dad deal with their grief, and they'd be there for him too. That's what family did.

There were a few relatives and family friends who I didn't recognise, but I wasn't bothered about them. I was keen to see which of my school friends had turned up. Leaving the coffin and my folks at the front of the funeral home, I wandered between the pews towards the back of the room. I could see Mrs Fulleylove, my form teacher, and, sitting beside her, Lucy Carpenter. Lucy's face was white, her eyes all red, like she'd been crying. Mrs Fulleylove had a consoling arm around her. She could clearly tell that Lucy had just lost the love of her life. That's what I was going with, anyway.

Lucy had a dozen of my classmates with her. Dougie was in the middle of them, deep into a whispered conversation with Andy Vaughn, another of our roleplaying game mates. Along with Stu Singer, they were the only ones I'd call proper friends – the rest had obviously taken the school up on the chance of missing a double German lesson. Melanie Shuker was there, the class mean girl, sobbing into a handkerchief. She looked terribly upset, which was odd. I'd barely said a word to her in the four years we'd been at High School together. I suppose German lessons can do that to you.

Stu Singer was the class clown, a daredevil and proper all-round mentalist. He was what you'd call a force of nature, although my old man had more choice words for him. A waste of talent really, as he was actually frighteningly smart, according to his grades. Simply put, intelligence and common sense don't always go hand in hand. As the founding (and sole) member of the Damage Squad, his duties included running around school shouting '*damage*' a lot, while tipping stacked chairs off tables or throwing yoghurt pots out of the third-floor windows of Upper School at passing Year Sevens. It wasn't hardcore vandalism by any means, but it clearly gave the unlikely rebel Stu a lot of satisfaction, especially considering his dad was a vicar. Indeed, Rev. Singer had run the proceedings an hour earlier at church, having been our family vicar throughout my life. As my nan would have said, it had been a lovely service, and all that was left now was the final curtain, so to speak.

There were no more speeches, all the kind words had been spoken back at St Mary's Church. Someone at the front of the funeral home hit *play* on the CD machine and a piece of classical music suddenly kicked in. This was most definitely not to my tastes. *I Am The Resurrection* by The Stone Roses would've been nice. Perhaps that'd make me spring back to life, leaping out of the coffin with jazz hands and shouting, 'Ta daa!' Like this was all a big joke I might wake up from at any moment. Talking of my coffin, when did they put the lid on it? Preoccupied spying on my friends as I had been, I didn't even see that happen. A curtain in the wall suddenly swung open, revealing a dark tunnel beyond. The coffin began to slide back along a bed of mechanical rollers, the music playing all the while, now accompanied by stifled sobs from my family and friends.

For the first time since the night of the accident I suddenly felt a sickening feeling hit me in the pit of my stomach. I'd found the whole business of fluttering around, eavesdropping on people's conversations and watching how my family dealt with their loss quite surreal. I'd been dipping in and out of the living world, as if awaking from naps to witness key moments as my body made its way inexorably down the home straight. The hospital, the church, the funeral home: I'd turned up in

15

time to watch proceedings, a spaced-out spectator who was forbidden from joining in. The closest thing I could liken the sensation to was when I'd foolishly raided my dad's drink cabinet with Dougie and Stu. I guess I'd felt drunk up until the moment the coffin moved. Now I just felt sick.

I didn't want to go. It was too soon. I hadn't had time to say goodbye to anybody. There was so much more I was going to do. I was going to learn how to speak French, to visit Paris. I was going to buy a Mini Cooper when I was old enough to drive – you can blame *The Italian Job* for that one. I was going to grow a bloody *moustache*!

I ran forward towards the front of the room as the head end of the coffin began to disappear into the wall, the tiny curtains rustling as the wooden sides brushed past. I tried to take hold of the polished brass handles, to slow the coffin's progress and buy a little more time, but my hands simply trailed through it, connecting with thin air, the box and my body continuing on their way. I started to panic now. I looked back at the room; nobody could see me . . .

Except Dougie.

Every face in the room was forlorn and tearful, seeing me off on my final journey. All except one. I could *swear* Dougie was staring *straight at me*. His jaw was slack and his eyes were wide, and his elbow was hammering into the ribs of Andy Vaughn at his side. He whispered something frantically into

Andy's ear, our friend following Dougie's gaze and squinting as he looked straight at me. He shook his head: negative. Whatever Dougie was looking at – that is, me – Andy couldn't see. Dougie's face drained of colour. I might have rushed over to him, if not for the pressing business of preventing my coffin from being swallowed up by the wall.

But then the curtain fell back into place with a pathetic *whoosh,* and I was left locked out, separated from my body. I could hear people rising from the pews behind me, going to speak to my parents and pass on their condolences. The stupid classical music kept playing on the funeral sound system – who chose that track anyway? More tunes flew through my head that I would have preferred: *Good Riddance* from Green Day perhaps? If I'd had my way I'd have been shuffling off the mortal coil to the accompaniment of The Clash – *Should I Stay Or Should I Go.* Though right now, it looked like I was staying, whether I wanted to or not.

FOUR

Thick and Thin

If you had to choose a location to live, there are a few places that would naturally make the top of the list. The flat above Domino's Pizza and the house across the street from Lucy Carpenter are givens, but a more imaginative mind might conjure up fancier settings. Swanky penthouses on top of skyscrapers, a house in the Hollywood Hills; those kind of things would be top of the heap. Next door to a graveyard would feature somewhere near the bottom, below a slaughterhouse but above a sewage farm.

Dougie had lived his entire life beside St Mary's cemetery, his bedroom window overlooking a sea of gravestones. As the crow flew, there was a shortcut I could take to Dougie's house from my own that would take me past our school and straight through the field of the dead. I never took it. I'd seen and read too many films and books to know that it was a risk not worth taking. It made far better sense to take the long route round, pretty much negating all possibility of being attacked by zombies. It added five minutes onto the journey but I'd always arrive in one piece.

Dead or alive had ceased to be a concern of late. I couldn't pinpoint the exact time I'd awoken after the funeral – the trauma of witnessing my own cremation had caused me to somehow black out – but I became slowly aware that I was at home again, my parents and brother having returned there after the wake. Mum had gone to bed early and Dad was downstairs, staring at the television, flicking mindlessly through the channels. I'd walked upstairs to Ben's room. He was online, chatting to his mates on Faceache. I hung over his shoulder for a moment, watching him reply to the sympathetic posts of his friends. He was having a private message conversation with his best mate, Sam. I felt like a bit of a snoop, spying on him as I was, but opportunities like this hadn't come around too often in life. I watched as Sam let Ben know he was thinking about him. I watched as Ben told him he loved him. *Loved him?* What the heck? When did this happen? How long had they been an item? Scratch that: how long had my brother been gay?

I was overwhelmed by guilt. Not just for eavesdropping on something as private as Ben and Sam's conversation, but for the fact that I truly didn't know my big brother at all. Had I ever known him?

'*Ben,*' I whispered, my lips millimetres from his ear, hoping for some kind of response. His fingers tapped away on the keyboard, his face showing no recognition or reaction whatsoever. I stepped back, retreating from the room and creeping into my parents' bedroom. Mum was trying to sleep. Her brow was knitted and furrowed, despair etched on to her face as she struggled to find refuge from the day's events. In her knuckled hands she still held my scarf, alongside my knackered old teddy, the one I'd had since I was born. He was missing an eye and his nose had worn away many years ago, but he'd always been the most precious toy I'd ever owned. Of course, I'd never have owned up to this when I was alive – this was a teddy, for flip's sake – but somehow he always managed to find himself on the foot of my bed. I'd been wearing the scarf the night I'd died. Mum had knitted it for me because I loved *Doctor Who*. She mistakenly thought that meant Tom Baker, the scarf-wearing fourth Doctor from the Seventies. It was still a groovy scarf. I glanced at my chest and there it was, oversized and overlong, still tied about my neck, trailing down to my knees. Mum never had been good at knitting, but it was the thought that counted.

Why was I still here? I moved away from Mum, not knowing where to turn. Surely I should have 'moved on' when my body went up in smoke? If I was stuck here, trapped in the living world, I needed to find out exactly how being dead worked.

I'd heard of ghosts having to stay in one place and haunt their own house for ever, but there was no way I was settling for that. I paused to look at my bedroom for one last time before heading out. Tatty posters on the wall, a cluttered bookshelf full of fantasy miniatures, books and CDs, an open wardrobe that looked like a bomb had hit it. Mum hadn't even bothered to make my bed. It was as I'd left it, a shrine to all that was me. I felt a strange, nagging sensation that I didn't belong here. I knew where I needed to go, where I belonged. I stepped through my bedroom wall, phasing through the brickwork, seemingly leaving my stomach behind in the process. I was learning fast – it seemed as though passing through solid objects made you feel as though you were going to throw up. If ghosts *can* throw up.

I took the route the crows flew, in the direction of Dougie's house. He had seen me, hadn't he, back in the funeral home? What are best mates for, if not to be there for you when you're dead? I pushed on through every obstacle that stood in my way – tree, gate, fence and phone box – battling through the nausea that came with it.

I passed our school, Brooklands, and thought of all the years I'd spent there, japing with my mates, fawning after

Lucy Carpenter, fleeing from bullies. Beside the school was Red Brook House, the predecessor of Brooklands. I paused to look at the monstrous mausoleum to a time long gone. Neighbourhood kids had always said the old condemned building, known locally as 'the House', was haunted. I'd scoffed at the notion. Until now. I stared at the ancient red brickwork, choked by dark ivy, creepers crawling through glassless windows. Although I felt no cold, I shivered. I left it behind, flitting across the playing fields as I raced into St Mary's cemetery.

There was nothing to scare me in the graveyard any more, so far as I knew, nor provide any obstacle. I found myself slowing, considering the words and epitaphs on the graves as I wandered between headstones and carved monuments of marble. There was the war memorial, the bright red garland of poppies at its base where old servicemen had placed it. I'd come here countless times with my local scout group, but never truly considered the sacrifice those lads had made decades – a century – ago. I traced my fingers over their names. I might have felt no physical connection, but something stirred in my heart. I walked past the memorial to the wall of remembrance, where the wreaths of the recently passed were placed. I recognised mine from my funeral instantly, my gurning portrait placed dead centre. There was a note from Mum and Dad attached: *Our beautiful boy, so sorely missed.* I choked up. Couldn't help myself. I needed to be out of the graveyard now. I set off at a pace.

I ran straight through the fence at the rear of the cemetery and skidded to a halt in Dougie's back garden. I paused for a moment to gather my senses and my stomach: the passing-through-solid-objects thing wasn't getting any easier, but I was sure as dammit going to master it. I could see the light on in Dougie's bedroom, could hear the hypnotic beat of his stereo. What was that he was listening to? One Direction? This had to be a cry for help. My hand wavered over the back door handle. *What was I thinking?* I stepped clean through it.

I passed the glass-panelled door to the living room, catching sight of Dougie's dad through the mottled glass, slumped in his armchair. Dougie's mum had passed away when he was little, his dad now the only family he had. Mr Hancock had always struck me as a sad soul, working awful hours as a driver for a local businessman and struggling to bring up his son alone. It was a miracle Dougie had grown up to be so well-rounded, and that was in no small part thanks to the love of his father. All the while the sound of Dougie's (disturbingly poor taste in) music drew me closer, my feet creeping up the stairs towards his bedroom. I stepped into Dougie's den, trying to ignore the odd sensation as I passed through the door.

He lay flat on his bed, feet hanging off the end and balancing on his drum-kit stool. His eyes were closed, hands resting on his belly, fingers drumming along to *Teenage Kicks*. He was still wearing the grey suit he'd worn at the funeral home, the tie yanked loose into a knot around his throat. I stood over him for a moment, trying to decide what to do, what to say. *Had he really seen me earlier? Was I just wasting my time?*

I opened my mouth to speak. 'Best mates through thick and thin?'

Any lingering concerns I'd had about whether Dougie had seen me vanished in an instant when he flicked open his eyes. He shrieked once – a sound familiar to anyone who's ever been suddenly and horribly surprised – before rolling off the bed, hitting the floor with a clumsy *thunk*. His stool tumbled forward, clattering into the drum-kit and sending his cymbals toppling over with a *clash*. When Dougie emerged from the other side of his bed he held his drumsticks in each hand, crossed over one another in the sign of the crucifix.

'Get back!' he cried, his face white with horror.

'This isn't *Buffy*, you idiot,' I said. 'I'm not a blood-sucking vampire.'

'Look . . . look at you!'

I lifted my hands, turning them over before my eyes. They were pale and deathly white, and with each movement they left a phosphorous blue shimmer trailing in the air. I looked like Ben Kenobi's spirit in *The Empire Strikes Back*, only instead of being aglow with Jedi magic it was the cold chill of death.

'Is everything all right up there, son?'

It was Mr Hancock, calling from the foot of the stairs. I stared at my best friend and shrugged.

'Your call, mate: *is* everything OK?'

Dougie chewed his lips, the drumsticks rattling against one another as he held them before him, warding me away.

'Fine thanks, Dad!' he called over his shoulder. He smiled, throwing me a hopeful look as if asking if he'd said the right thing.

'Dougie, I'm still Will. I haven't changed that much.'

'Haven't changed?' gasped Dougie, killing the stereo with a flick of a switch. 'You're dead.'

'But I'm still me. Anyway, you can talk about change: One Direction? What's with that?'

'It was on the radio.'

'I can *see* the CD box, dude!'

Dougie glowered at me as the thumping of footsteps on the stairs warned us that his dad was on his way up to investigate.

'You're a flippin' *ghost*, Will!'

'You saw me this afternoon, Dougie, back at the funeral home. You've got to see; I've nowhere else to go.'

'Your folks live over the way: can't you go there?'

'You don't understand, mate. I've been there, but it just felt wrong. They were all so sad, so miserable. I couldn't be near them.' I shrugged. 'I'd rather just hang out.'

The door opened and the haggard face of Mr Hancock appeared around the corner.

'Are you sure you're all right, Douglas?'

I was standing directly between father and son. Ordinarily, this might obscure the line of sight of one to the other, but that wasn't really a problem any more. Dougie looked straight through me towards his dad as his old man smiled back sadly.

'Yes . . . thanks, Dad,' whispered Dougie. 'I'm just tired.'

'It's been an exhausting time, son, for you as much as anyone. Don't make it a late one, eh? You've got school tomorrow.'

Dougie's dad's pale face was etched with concern, the worry lines more pronounced than ever. He didn't look well at all, clearly my loss and its effect on his son having hit him hard too. Mr Hancock was Dougie's sole caregiver and still treated him like a kid, though his heart was definitely in the right place. Now he pulled the door closed, leaving the two of us alone once more.

'I completely forgot it was school tomorrow,' I said, sitting down beside Dougie on the end of his bed.

'I know: double science first thing. I hate Thursdays.'

'You're not alone,' I sighed.

Dougie did a double-take suddenly.

'This is insane, Will. You're a ghost! Why are you here?'

'I thought that once they'd shoved me in the oven at the funeral home I'd be on my way, but I appear to be stuck here.'

Dougie laughed.

'The oven. I like that.' Then as he remembered the gravity of the situation he added: 'Sorry, mate.'

'Forget it.'

'So how does this ghost thing work? Are you not destined to haunt your own family for all eternity?'

'No, thank God, and I can't say that's not a relief! It's not much fun there right now.'

'How about the graveyard? Surely that's where you belong?'

'Nope, apparently not. I didn't get stuck there either.'

'What are we going to do?' asked Dougie, shaking his head, still struggling to believe the strange turn of events.

'Well, for starters, you're going to go to school tomorrow.'

'And what will you do?'

'Reckon I'll start the day with double science.'

'Huh?'

I smiled and shook my wrists, jazz-hands stylee.

'I'm coming with you!'

FIVE

Design and Technology

'He's standing next to you *right now*?'

Stu Singer's face had never been more animated. His eyes were wide and his grin looked like it might tear his face in two. Dougie nodded as Stu slapped a hand to his brow and shook his forehead.

'This is mad!'

'Are you sure you can't see him?' asked Dougie.

Stu pointed directly at me.

'He's here?'

Dougie nodded again, as Stu threw his hand out, his fingers passing straight through me harmlessly. Stu sent a punch my way next, the fist disappearing into where my stomach should have been but connecting with nothing. He threw a few more punches and karate chops as Dougie and I looked at one another, unimpressed. I stepped away, walking round the other side of Dougie, leaving Stu to knock lumps out of thin air.

'So *nobody* can see me except you?'

'Seems that way,' whispered Dougie as he watched Stu effortlessly unbalance himself with a high kick that sent him tumbling to the floor of the wood-store. Mr Russell, our design and technology teacher, was oblivious to our presence in the storeroom. So long as he had a bit of wood to whittle away at on the lathe in the machine-room, he was happy.

'Did I get him?' asked Stu from the linoleum.

'Yeah, you got him,' lied Dougie, turning away.

I stepped past Stu, who was clambering back to his feet, and joined Dougie by the window that overlooked the schoolyard. Clouds of dead leaves swirled through the air, tiny twisters of red, yellow and brown whirling across the play-ground.

'They're going to think I'm mad, you know,' he said.

'Why's that?'

'All these conversations I'm having with myself. I look and sound like a proper nutter. Cheers for that, you div!'

'They can't see me; they can't hear me. You're the only one who's paying me any attention. You're the special one, D!'

'So special that I get to be haunted by my best mate? Winner!' he said, punching his fist feebly in the air.

'You know what, Dougie,' said Stu, having now righted himself, 'my dad could take care of this for you. He's a vicar, remember? Man of the cloth and all that. He knows stuff.' Stu stepped up and whispered, possibly trying to ensure that I couldn't hear him: 'He can make Will go away.'

'He does realise I'm standing *right here,* doesn't he?' I said.

'What do you mean?' Dougie asked Stu. 'You make it sound like Will's one of the Sopranos.'

'Dad can exorcise him.'

'He can do that?'

'Oi!' I shouted, my annoyance rising at an alarming rate. I might have been in limbo but I had a lot of questions that needed answering. I didn't need Stu's dad throwing holy water or whatever my way.

'Deffo, he's down with all that stuff, possessions and what-not. Mate of his in Liverpool saw a bloke levitate once. They're like Ghostbusters, these priests and vicars.'

'Please tell me you've stopped listening to him,' I said, as Stu's imagination bounded off into la-la-land. Stu was famous for telling everyone that his grandpa was in the SAS when he really worked for Parcel Force. He was terribly bright and had a photographic memory, but for all those smarts, he was strangely naive. It was rumoured his stupidity would be the death of him. I thought Stu was an idiot savant, although Dougie reckoned he was just a common or garden idiot.

'Exorcising? I thought that was only in the movies,' said Dougie.

'Nobody's going to exorcise anybody!' I shouted, my temper fraying. I struck out at Dougie and although I didn't feel my hand connect, to my surprise I saw his shoulder bounce a little, as if gently patted.

He and I looked at his shoulder, both shocked by the apparent connection, and stared at one another. Stu walked through me as he made his way out of the wood-store and back into the design and technology classroom. A wave of nausea rippled through me with his passing.

'Gimme a shout when you make your mind up, bro,' he said to Dougie as he strutted off, knocking over a wood-pile in true Damage Squad fashion. 'I ain't afraid of no ghosts . . .'

'So you felt that?' I asked excitedly when Stu had gone.

'I felt . . . something.'

'But you moved your shoulder when I lashed out.'

'I saw you swing. Perhaps it was instinct? An impulse reaction?'

That wasn't the answer I needed to hear. If I could *touch* something in the real world, then what else might I be capable of?

'No, there's got to be more to it than that. There's a way I can connect with the living world. I just know it. I just need to tap into that. Find out how to . . .'

I noticed Dougie was staring out of the window, paying me little attention. A group of girls were making their way across the schoolyard and there, at the back of them, was Lucy Carpenter.

'I wonder if she can see me,' I whispered.

'I doubt it,' said Dougie.

I shivered. Dougie's words had struck a chord. There was something I had to tell him. Something had slipped my mind. I was close to remembering what that was when Mr Russell interrupted.

'Hancock,' he said, catching Dougie by surprise.

I wondered how long the teacher had been standing there.

'Yes, sir?'

'I think you might need to have a talk with someone, young man,' he said, reaching out and patting Dougie on the shoulder.

Dougie glanced at me, rolling his eyes as Russell led him back to his desk, muttering something about the school nurse and post-traumatic stress disorder.

SIX

Head and Heart

Dougie sat slouched in the chair outside Mr Goodman's office, Drumstick Lolly in mouth, feet tapping nervously on the carpet. The lolly made him look nerdier than ever. It had been a parting gift from the Mrs Jolly, the appropriately-named school nurse. Mrs Jolly was a lovely, plump, roly-poly lady with cheeks the colour – and texture – of strawberries. She was without doubt the one person you wanted to see if you had any ailment, from a grazed knee to a broken arm, such was her ability to put one's mind at ease. Invariably a key component of all her medical remedies would be a lollipop, doled out from an enormous tub she kept on top of her filing cabinet. The lollies were a leftover from her previous job in a primary school.

You can't underestimate the healing powers of a good lolly, regardless of your age. Dougie had devoured one while he'd sat with her, as she talked him through bereavement and depression. He'd left the room with two more stashed in his pocket, the first of which had already found its way into his mouth as he waited for the headmaster to call him in.

'Why does he want to see you?' I asked as we stared at Goodman's door.

'Hang on a minute. I'll just turn on my psychic link.'

Mrs Jolly appeared down the corridor, passing from her office to the staffroom, winking and throwing Dougie a thumbs-up as she went by.

'She's ace, isn't she?' said Dougie quietly, keeping our chats as secretive as possible after the nurse's pep-talk. 'I wish she was my mum.'

'You really want to consult your dad on that before you marry them off. He might have something to say on the matter. She's twice his size!'

Dougie smiled.

'A diet of Drumsticks and Double Lollies will do that.'

We both laughed as the headmaster's door opened.

'What's so funny, Hancock?'

Goodman was a tall, rangy man, with an award-winning comb-over that swept across his bald head. Legend said it was backcombed up from his bum, though nobody was about to investigate. He always wore the same brown tweed jacket with leather arm patches, and mismatched trousers.

'Nothing sir,' said Dougie, recovering his composure instantly.

'Hmm,' said Goodman, standing to one side. 'In you come, boy.'

I hummed the tune to the Imperial March from *Star Wars* as I followed them into the office, blissfully aware that my tomfoolery might set Dougie off again at any moment. I saw his shoulders shake a little as he sat down in front of Goodman's desk, the headmaster settling on the other side and leaning back in his leather captain's chair. His father's old mining pick and lantern sat on one shelf of his enormous bookshelf, a reminder of where he'd come from. Goodman was big on tradition and roots. You can take the man out of Yorkshire, etcetera.

'You're not in trouble, Hancock, but you can lose the lollipop for starters.'

Dougie whipped the sweet out of his mouth and sat up straight. Goodman took the school very seriously, commanding respect from pupils and staff alike. You could often find him striding around the school on his spindly legs, barking orders like that demented bloke from *Fawlty Towers*. Parents, naturally, loved him.

'I wanted to see you because I've been ... made aware of your circumstances.'

'I don't follow, sir.'

35

'This talking and muttering to yourself, boy: there've been a couple of mentions in the staffroom this morning, and now Mrs Jolly has got me up to speed. I just wanted to say, Hancock: we can make sure you get help, should you need it.'

It was at this point in time that ordinarily I might have whispered something insensitive regarding a trip to the loony bin, but it suddenly didn't seem like such a good idea. Looking at it from the school's perspective, one of their pupils was coming apart at the seams after a seriously traumatic experience. Dougie was having a tough enough time dealing with me being a ghost – now he had to convince the school that he wasn't mad.

'I'm all right, sir. Really.'

'You sure?' Goodman leaned over his desk, fingers knitting together as he whispered conspiratorially. 'Don't feel you have to bottle things up, Hancock. The best thing to do is talk about your feelings, understand?'

Dougie nodded, eyes wide and unblinking. This was Goodman trying to 'be friendly', and it reminded me an awful lot of a dog attempting to miaow. In all the years I'd been at school, the headmaster had been many things, but friendly wasn't one of them. Intimidation was more his style, a fierce glare that commanded respect and produced toilet-related mishaps for those pupils with the weakest bladders. Dougie and I were used to Goodman's gruff act now, so seeing him trying to play the 'nice card' was slightly unnerving.

I walked around the headmaster's desk – out of habit, really, as I could just as easily have strode through it – and across to the window. I really did feel like I was eavesdropping now. I shouldn't be in here with Dougie as he had a heart-to-heart with Goodman. Maybe there *was* something Dougie wanted to say, but couldn't with me being present. I glanced back and hooked my thumb towards the window, mouthing the question: 'Want me to go?'

Dougie shook his head.

'There's really nothing you want to talk about, boy?' With his dickie-bows and cravats, Goodman looked more like Doctor Who's dad than a headmaster, but you wouldn't dare ask him where he'd parked his TARDIS.

'Not really, sir. Me and Will were best mates, and I guess . . . I don't know what I'm thinking at the moment. I'm not sure what I'm supposed to feel.'

'You're struggling to deal with the loss, aren't you? It's perfectly natural to grieve, Hancock.'

If only it were that easy for Dougie, I thought. I was right there, I wasn't going anywhere. If I *was* gone he could start to deal with it, but I was still there for him, and he was still there for me. *Best mates through thick and thin.* And through life and death . . .

I caught sight of Mr Borley, the school caretaker, raking the grass outside Goodman's office window. Autumn was the busiest time of year for the old man, with every tree in the neighbourhood managing to dump its dead leaves onto his yards and playing fields. With a thick mop of greying hair on his head and mutton-chop sideburns, he reminded me of old photos of Dad I'd seen in the family album. Dad had been a bit of a rocker in his youth. Only he'd grown out of it. Didn't look like Borley ever had. He glanced up towards me suddenly. Instinctively, I ducked out of sight.

He couldn't see me, could he? I looked back at Dougie, who raised an eyebrow as if to say, *What are you hiding from? You're a ghost, stupid!*

I stepped back to the window behind Goodman's chair and peered out again. There was Borley, bent over his rake, seemingly oblivious. I shivered – ridiculous, I know, considering I was dead, but it was a deep-rooted nervous reaction. Something wasn't quite right about Borley, but I didn't know what.

'I'm looking out for you, boy,' said Goodman, standing up and walking to the door. 'I want you to know that.'

He opened it as Dougie rose from his chair and turned to make his way out of the room. As my pal passed him, Goodman dipped into the chest pocket of Dougie's blazer and whipped out the final lollipop.

'Oh, Drumstick!' he grinned. 'My favourite.'

Goodman patted my friend on the back and propelled him out of the door, with me ghosting past in hot pursuit.

'And remember, Hancock,' he said as he shut the door, his voice echoing from beyond as he finished the sentence, 'my door's always open.'

SEVEN

Gardens and Graveyards

'What on earth are you *doing?*'

Dougie jumped up in bed, suddenly awake, drawing his duvet up under his chin in shock.

'Oh, don't be so overdramatic,' I said, waving his protestations away. 'I was only watching you while you slept.'

'Watching me sleep?' he wheezed. 'Oh, well that's a relief. For a moment I thought you might be doing something *really* creepy.'

'Creepy would be those underpants you're wearing: The Incredible Hulk? How old are you again?'

'They were a gift.'

'When you were seven? Reckon you should've moved on by now ...'

'Can *we* move on, please? How do we get you to where you

need to be? And by that I'm talking about the Great Hereafter or wherever it is you belong. You can't stay perched on the foot of my bed like some phantom parrot, pal.'

'Sorry to freak you out, buddy, but it's not exactly a cake-walk for me either!'

'Can't you go and haunt Lucy Carpenter or something?'

'Believe me, the last place I want to be is stuck in your room playing Casper the Friendly Ghost while you snore and fart your way to sunrise.'

'Then why *are* you here?'

I had to think for a moment: it was a fair question. What was it that had drawn me to Dougie? I'd bimbled around his bedroom while he snored, eventually settling at the foot of his bed. And I'd been quite content there. I can't say I'd slept – ghosts don't sleep, I'd learned that very early on – but I felt at peace. Why had I stayed in his room, crouched over him like some spectral simpleton? There were certainly other places I'd much rather have been: his suggestion of haunting Lucy Carpenter wasn't a bad one at all.

'I wish I could tell you, mate, but I haven't the foggiest idea. This limbo gig doesn't come with a handbook!'

'Then perhaps somebody should write one,' said Dougie.

'I'll dictate, you take notes.'

We grinned momentarily before I continued.

'Well, there's nobody showing me the ropes. I really can't put my finger on it, only to say that being here feels ... right. Can't be any clearer than that, as I really don't get it yet. As for what I *should* be doing, who knows? What do your other ghost mates usually do?'

Dougie clicked his fingers, jumping out of bed and rushing to his bedroom window. Yanking the curtains back, he looked out into the night.

'You might be on to something. There must be others like you.'

'Others?'

'Phantoms, lost souls, ghosts and ghouls; you can't be alone.'

I joined him at the windowsill, our eyes searching the nearby cemetery. During the day it was a peaceful, restful place, a shortcut to school for many kids. At night, however, a transformation took place. Gravestones jutted from the thin mist like trolls' teeth, beyond the back garden fence. It looked like the perfect setting for a haunting, a grim world of gloom and shadows, straight out of a horror movie.

'Do you really believe you're on your own? You can't be the only restless spirit out there.'

'What are you suggesting?'

'Let me grab a torch,' said Dougie, dashing to the foot of his bed.

'And your jeans,' I suggested, catching an unwelcome glimpse of the unsightly superhero pants as he pulled on his trainers.

A loose fence panel enabled Dougie to slip from his garden through to the graveyard, while I simply stepped through the thin timber and materialised on the other side. I was gradually getting used to the sensation – moving swiftly was the best way to avoid nausea. Though not having a stomach to hurl with certainly helped. Still, going too slowly made my eyes feel like onions, layer after layer peeling away as I passed through.

'So, what are we looking for exactly?' I whispered as I moved alongside my friend, the two of us scouring the darkness for anything supernatural.

'You tell me,' he replied. 'I assumed you'd be all tuned in to whatever frequency ghosts work on.'

'It's not like Bluetooth, you know? I'm learning on the job!'

'You can't see them?'

'Tell you what, the minute I do, I'll let you know.'

'What, you're a ghost who can't see ghosts?'

'I've no idea, I've never done this before!'

'Have to say, mate,' muttered Dougie, 'your haunting leaves a lot to be desired. Mooching about all day and night hardly strikes me as constructive use of your afterlife. You should be out hooking up with some more ghostly folk.'

'Of course,' I said, rolling my eyes. 'I just need to put my name down for Afterlife Anonymous, get along to the next meeting.'

'I just think if you'd been searching for some other spirits you might be a little further along by now, uncovering why you're here. They could help you move on.'

'There you go again, saying you want me to move on,' I replied.

'Well, don't *you* want to?'

I shrugged. 'I don't reckon I do. This is my second bite of the apple: I doubt I'll get another one. If I move on, as you put it, I'm gone for good.'

'So I'm stuck with you for the foreseeable?'

'I love you too, big guy,' I smiled.

'Which brings us back to what's actually keeping you here.'

'Isn't it obvious? I'm still here because I need to find the driver of the car that killed me. It has to be that.'

'It *has* to be that?' exclaimed Dougie, stopping in the mist beside a gnarled old tree. 'I thought it was love that kept spirits from moving on.'

That was when it came to me, like a lightning bolt out of the blue. The nagging sensation at the back of my mind, that important thing that I had needed to tell Dougie on the night of my death: I had remembered it. The trauma must have buried the memory.

'Lucy Carpenter kissed me.'

Naturally, my revelation caused Dougie to halt in his tracks, as if hit by an elephant gun.

'You lying git,' he said. 'You've more chance of snatching a smooch off Mrs Jolly!'

'It's the truth!'

'It's a head trauma,' scoffed Dougie. 'That car hit you hard, dude!'

I shook my head, growing more confident with every passing second as my memory returned. The smirk gradually grew into a grin.

'You think I'd lie about a kiss? What do I stand to gain?'

'My undying admiration because you snogged the school hottie, for starters.'

'Enough with the undying,' I said, suddenly finding a spring in my stride. For the first time since my death, I was beginning to feel positive. 'Look, I can't find any other way of explaining this, but the answer to why I'm a ghost is directly connected to that night. I think it's discovering the truth that's keeping me here.'

Dougie glanced around the gravestones, casting his torch about in sweeping arcs. It was clear to the pair of us that the cemetery was devoid of supernatural activity. Whoever the dead beneath our feet were, it was clear they were resting in peace.

'This is rubbish,' he said. 'We won't be finding any answers tonight: there's nothing here. If there are ghosts out there, we're going to have to cast our net wider to catch one.'

'Catch one? Are you a Ghostbuster now? Don't get all Venkman on me.'

'I ain't afraid of no ghost! Not if they're all like you, anyway. I've seen scarier episodes of *Scooby-Doo*.'

'There's nothing scarier than those underpants.'

'Don't diss the growlers, pal!' said Dougie, turning on his heel and promptly tripping over an upturned root hidden beneath the mist. The root suddenly moved, leading to a frightened yowl from my friend as he scrambled backwards. A dark shape ran between the graves, its fleshy tail snaking behind it as the creature fled from the teenager.

'Ain't afraid of ghosts, but a rat makes you scream like a girl!'

'Shut it, Casper!' said Dougie, scrambling to his feet, mud covering his dressing gown as it flapped open in the breeze. 'I hate rats, as well you know!'

'I think you just soiled the Hulk,' I laughed. 'Way to make him angry!'

EIGHT

Dungeons and Dragons

'I'm not joking, Andy,' said Stu Singer, reaching across the table to grab a slice of pizza. 'He's being haunted by Will!'

Andy Vaughn, Dungeon Master of our small band of geeks, glanced up wearily and shook his head.

'For a clever lad you can be extremely gullible, Stu. He's pulling your leg. Tell him, Dougie, and put the idiot out of his misery.'

'Can we just get back to the game, please?' said Dougie, trying to change the subject as he picked up the die and rolled it across the table. The twenty-sided gem bounced off the pizza box and rattled to a halt. Andy leaned forward from behind his Dungeon Master's screen, peering over the edge of his glasses to inspect the roll.

'Seven. That's a fail. You've picked the chest's lock all right, but you feel something sharp prick your thumb.'

Stu laughed at Dougie's misfortune, showing the true camaraderie that provided the heart of every adventuring party in the world of roleplaying games. 'Can I have a look at what's inside?' he said, showing more interest in the chest's contents than the injury Dougie's halfling thief had sustained.

'Watch him,' I whispered. 'He'll nick the lot.'

'Hang on a minute,' exclaimed Dougie. 'Can we just resolve what's happened to me before you loot the chest? I get first dibs as it was me who picked the lock, remember?'

Stu leaned back in his chair, waving his pizza slice triumphantly. 'You go for it, Dougie. I can wait until you're dead.'

'You're supposed to be a blooming cleric, aren't you?' grumbled Dougie. 'You're the worst holy man I've ever met!'

'So Stu is saying you're being haunted by Will?' asked Andy. 'Do you remember when he spent an entire summer telling everyone dwarves don't have knees?'

'They don't!' exclaimed Stu.

'They do, Stu,' replied Dougie with a sly grin. 'But you can thank Will for that one. It was his idea to tell you that.'

'Thanks, Will,' said Stu into thin air.

'No worries,' I said, knowing he wouldn't hear me.

'Will says, "*No worries*",' said Dougie, passing on my comment.

While Stu smiled to be acknowledged by me, Andy laughed, forgetting the game and staring at Dougie incredulously.

'You *genuinely* think that the spirit of Will came back from the dead? Why on earth would he bother haunting *you?*'

'We don't know,' said Dougie, spinning the odd-shaped dice on the table. 'Reckons he's got unfinished business.'

'Dude, you're as gullible as Stu!'

'It's true,' sighed Dougie. 'He's here with me now. He's *always* here.'

I didn't miss the hint of annoyance in Dougie's voice. Fond of each other though we were, we hadn't been apart since the evening after my cremation – that never sounds any less ridiculous – and it was clear my presence was wearing him down. I felt bad, but what could I do? For whatever reason, I'd gravitated toward my friend. I was drawn to him as sure as a pensioner goes for a profiterole. If anything, the more time we'd spent in one another's company, the stronger that bond had become, to such a point that I felt nauseous at the prospect of being apart from Dougie. I was drawing strength from my best mate, there were no two ways about it.

'Will? An ever-present phantasm?' Andy shook his head. 'No, I'm not having that. I need proof.'

I stepped around the table and looked at the open rulebook in front of him, obscured from the others by his cardboard screen. A quick glance over Andy's shoulder at the contents on the page gave me all the information I needed.

'Tell him he's on page forty-seven of the rulebook and that the chest's booby-trapped with a poison dart which will kill when you fail a saving throw. Tell him also that the chest contains eighty-one gold pieces, a giant ruby, a bottomless bag of holding and a gauntlet of smiting. Also tell him he's got a humungous zit on the back of his neck. I'd stand well clear if I were you.'

Dougie recounted this information to Andy, embellishing the last fact by saying I'd described the zit as a volcano ready to blow. Andy winced as he ran his hand nervously across his neck, examining the rulebook before him. The colour came fast to his cheeks.

'You must have this book or something, that's the only explanation,' he said in a fluster.

'No,' said Dougie. 'It's *not* the only explanation, is it? Will's here, with us right now, and he's going nowhere.'

'And what's the unfinished business which is keeping him here?' asked Andy, warily warming to the idea.

'Perhaps it's love?' offered Dougie with a sly wink to me. 'He always had the hots for Lucy Carpenter.'

'He had *no* chance with Lucy Carpenter,' scoffed Andy as I sneered at them. 'It's got to be something else.'

'Revenge,' said Stu, polishing off another slice of pizza. The other two turned to him.

'What?' asked Andy.

'Revenge for whoever killed him. The driver of that car just drove off. Not having justice is often what keeps a ghost from moving on, at least in many of the stories I've read.'

Stu slurped the pizza sauce from his fingers as the three of us stared at him. Even I was impressed by this rare show of insight from him. Stu had a habit of hitting us with observations, facts and trivia when we least expected it, and we rather liked it. It kept us on our toes.

'See,' I said to Dougie. 'I told you: that's why I'm still here.'

Dougie shook his head and turned to Andy. 'What would you do if you were being haunted?'

'Probably see about getting an exorcism or something.'

'Hang about,' I said. 'That's going a bit far, isn't it?'

'Isn't that just for evil spirits?' asked Dougie, ignoring me. 'Will might've been guilty of having dodgy haircuts and a hand-me-down wardrobe, but it'd be a push to describe him as evil. Where would we even start?'

'Like I said, speak to my dad,' said Stu, devouring the last pizza slice before anyone could bagsy it. 'He's a vicar, after all. Or maybe try a medium.'

'Don't you feel bad classing your old man in with nutters who think they can speak to spirits?' asked Andy.

'Father or palm reader, it's all the same to me,' replied Stu. 'There's that girl at school who reckons she's got the gift – Bloody Mary. I bet she can help you.'

'I wouldn't if I were you. She's a right weirdo,' muttered Andy. 'How do you know so much about the Queen of Darkness, then?'

'She and I went to the same dance class in juniors.'

'You were in a dance class?' we all said in unison.

'I'm a man of mystery,' came Stu's reply.

'I'm torn between which is the scarier image,' said Andy. 'You or her in a leotard.'

'I've told you nerds before, any questions about girls, come and see me,' he replied.

'Sounds like you're keen on Bloody Mary,' said Dougie.

'Nah, no way.' He grinned. 'Wouldn't touch her with a ten-foot bargepole.'

'Can we get back to the more pressing business of Will haunting me?' said Dougie. 'So your dad might be able to help us? Does he do exorcisms?'

'Dunno. Reckon he'll have a go though. I'm pretty sure he's seen the film, *The Exorcist*. How hard can it be?'

'I don't *need* exorcising!' I shouted, though only Dougie responded, with a mischievous grin.

'Are you going to roll this saving throw or what?' asked Stu, getting bored and tossing the greasy gem die to Dougie.

'I think we'll pass on the exorcism for now,' replied Dougie. He rolled the die and the four of us watched its twenty sides spin to a halt.

Andy sucked his teeth as they crowded around the resultant roll. 'Yikes. That's going to hurt. A lot. If it's any consolation, the poison's extremely fast acting and Filo Bigfoot, halfling pickpocket extraordinaire, is dead within a minute.'

Stu patted Dougie on the back.

'Bad luck, mate,' he said, before turning to Andy with a manic grin, grimacing as he spied the Dungeon Master's neck. 'Now then, Spotty, about that gauntlet of smiting . . .'

NINE

Shock and Awe

'Are you sure this'll work?' asked Dougie, forcing his hair into clumpy spikes before the mirror.

'Honestly. PVA is the next best thing to hair gel, just peels right out after it dries. I saw it on *Art Attack* once.'

With the lower school toilets to ourselves, Dougie was taking a moment to look the part before sidling up to Bloody Mary. With his hair now resembling that of a pocket punk, we were ready to roll.

'One more thing,' he said, daubing his eyelids with a smear of marker pen. Two black flashes completed my friend's gothic transformation with a minimum of fuss.

'How do I look?'

'I believe the expression is *well dark*, although you don't see many goths wearing parka coats.'

'I've told you. The coat stays. It's my signature fashion statement.'

'That statement being *I belong in the Seventies.*'

Dougie slouched out of the toilets, heading for the playground, me shadowing his every step. It'd been a funny weekend for the pair of us, a few contentious issues resolved. I'd agreed *not* to sit over Dougie's bed any more, and in return he'd promised to throw away his Hulk underpants.

'I still say this isn't the right thing to do,' I said.

'Why?'

'You're barking up the wrong tree with Mary. We should be trying to find out who was behind the wheel of the car.'

'I disagree,' said Dougie with a shake of his spiky head. 'If she's the real deal, she'll know what's what. She'll help you move on.'

'There you go again, banging on about helping me pass over!'

'I thought that's what you wanted?'

'Mate, you're proposing killing me all over again!'

'I'm trying to *help* you, Will,' he countered.

'Whatever,' I grumbled as we continued on our way.

Bloody Mary was a Year Eleven student and known by pretty much everyone in school as *the* resident kook. There were plenty of pupils who were into the alternative scenes, from the gangs of skate kids and parkour nuts who made the precinct their own after dark, to the maudlin goths who gathered on the park benches. They'd always amused me and Dougie the most: the majority of them came from well-to-do families and had everything handed to them on a plate. They wouldn't know stress or real drama if it bit them on their skinny-jeaned bums. It was all image over substance. I bet *I* had more Cure albums than the lot of them put together! There was surely more to being a *real* goth than wearing stripy oversize jumpers, listening to Green Day and gushing about Tim Burton movies . . . but Bloody Mary was about to show us the true meaning of the word.

'Do you really reckon she's got the sixth sense?' I asked Dougie as he headed across the yard towards Mary's hangout.

'We'll know soon enough . . .'

'I *see dead geeks,*' I whispered as we sloped off behind the bike sheds.

Mary had a smoker's cough to rival that of a coalminer, and her hacking gave her away before we saw her. A good head taller than Dougie and twice as broad, she cut an imposing figure. Her trenchcoat made her look like she'd misplaced her U-boat, the long black leather hanging down to her Doc Martens. Purple fingernails gripped a roll-up fag that wept its filthy smoke into the air around her. A shock of bright red hair exploded from her scalp.

As Dougie advanced she looked up, glowering at my friend

as if he'd just thrown a fistful of dog muck in her face. I couldn't shake David Attenborough's voice from my head, imagining my favourite TV naturalist describing a male spider approaching a black widow. Nothing about Bloody Mary was welcoming – a zombie would've provided a warmer embrace. I waved awkwardly, nervously, half expecting her to acknowledge me – she was meant to have 'the sight' after all. If she did see me, she paid no attention, her suspicious glare fixed on poor Dougie.

'Bloody Mary, isn't it?' he asked rather obviously as he leaned awkwardly against the wall. Dougie was playing it as cool as he could, staring off into space, avoiding eye contact. He probably thought this made him look mysterious and enigmatic. In fact it made him look rude and cocky, and Mary's face told its own tale. Ordinarily I might have tried to warn him that he was heading for a beating, but since he was planning on having me exorcised I decided to wait and see how this played out. OK, so perhaps I was slightly evil after all.

'Do I know you, scrote?' she asked, blowing smoke at him. The cloud engulfed Dougie, causing him to splutter as he replied, turning at last to the older girl.

'The name's Nosebleed,' he said, his voice breaking just enough to undermine his goth credentials. He was only half lying: Dougie did gain the nickname 'Nosebleed' in Year

Seven, but that was down to a dizzy spell on The Big One at Blackpool, rather than any great street-fighting prowess. There were cooler ways of earning such a nickname, for sure.

'Never heard of you.'

Dougie did a slow blink, revealing his dark warpaint.

'I know you, though,' he replied nonchalantly, 'and I know what you can do.'

Again with the glare.

'And what *can* I do?'

'You can speak to the dead.'

'Who told you that?'

'Any true goth knows you're the real deal,' Dougie said, hitting her with his best compliment.

'Why are you so interested, Nosebleed?'

'I've a friend who died,' said Dougie, as if it were the most natural thing in the world. She clicked her fingers in sudden recognition.

'*Now* I know you. You were mates with that lad who got killed by the hit-and-run, right?' she asked, news of my death having clearly reached the darkest corners of the school.

'I still am,' he replied. 'He's stuck here and doesn't know how to move on.'

'I don't *want* to move on,' I interjected, but Dougie carried on regardless.

'I figured you might know how to make that happen.'

'He's here *now*?' she said, looking around.

'She's staring straight through me, mate,' I whispered to Dougie.

'You can't see him?' he asked.

Mary shrugged. 'I can reach the departed . . . sometimes. I just need to be in the right mood.'

'I could help you with that,' said Dougie. 'I mean, getting you in the mood.'

'You could, could you?' she said huskily, her voice as smooth as broken glass. I don't think Dougie realised what he'd just said.

'Yeah, whatever you need, I'm there,' said Dougie, his gothic mask slipping as his natural exuberance came to the fore. 'How are you fixed tonight? My dad's gonna be out so we won't be interrupted.'

Bloody Mary was smiling now, her tobacco-stained teeth shining dully from between her black lips.

'Give us your address,' she said, as Dougie rifled through his blazer to grab his marker pen and a used bus ticket. Scribbling the details down on the scrap of paper, he handed it over, waving the black pen in the air with a rather-chuffed grin.

'My eyeliner,' he said. 'Never leave home without it!'

'That?' she replied, nodding approvingly as she pocketed the ticket. 'Hardcore, Nosebleed. I'll see you later. After dark.'

With that she was off, shambling further into the shadow world behind the bike sheds like a behemoth. There she would wait, shrouded by darkness and biding her time, at least until the bell went and she had to go to food technology. Dougie waved his marker victoriously in my face.

'Hardcore, she called me! We'll have this sorted this evening, mate, mark my words.'

'I hope you know what you're doing, Nosebleed,' I muttered, staring ruefully at the pen in his hand.

'Why's that?'

'That eyeliner you've just applied is permanent marker.'

TEN

Kiss and Tell

'I can't believe you've left her alone in your bedroom,' I said as Dougie banged the fridge door shut with his bum, a couple of cans in his hands. 'She's probably rifling through your drawers at the moment, sifting through your smalls. Are you sure you binned those Hulk growlers?'

'Very funny, Casper,' Dougie muttered, walking straight through me as he made for the hall.

'That's very rude, you know?' I called after him, quick to follow. 'Ghosts have feelings too!'

With Mr Hancock out for the evening at the local pub quiz, the stage was set for Bloody Mary's dark arts. I should probably say I felt entirely safe from the prospect of exorcism when she couldn't even see me. I was convinced the only way for me to move on would be to uncover the mysteries of my death. Mary had more chance of growing a pair of bat wings than banishing me to the Great Hereafter. Dougie seemed cool with this too. I could be a pest, but he didn't really want to see me gone. He too wanted to get to the bottom of why I was here, and he was convinced Mary was the real deal. Me? I had doubts. Lots of them.

The air was thick with tension. Mary had arrived looking sombre and otherworldly, as though she'd just been beamed down on to the doorstep from her mothership. She'd changed ever so slightly from her attire at school, black lipstick shifting to blood red while a big silver hoop had appeared through her nostrils. Standing to one side, Dougie had ushered her in, checking her preference for drinks. When he'd told her Southern Comfort was not actually an option, she'd reluctantly agreed to try some Dandelion and Burdock, before stomping up the stairs and into Dougie's room. And there she waited, as my friend climbed the stairs towards her, his hands trembling with trepidation at the evening ahead.

'What are you worried about? She's only here for a bit of light exorcism,' I joked as Dougie headed upstairs. He stumbled as he climbed, almost dropping the cans as he regathered his footing.

'I've never had a girl in my bedroom before,' he hissed before arriving on the landing, nudging his door open with a tentative toe-poke.

'You've never had a girl in your *house*,' I corrected him sympathetically.

The first thing to hit us as we entered his bedroom was the pall of smoke that now hung in the air, Mary having wasted no time in sparking up. She was sitting at the foot of his bed, back against the wall, casting her eyes over the plethora of Warhammer posters that cluttered his walls. To my horror, I spied her using one of Dougie's chess club cups as an ash tray. I knew how dear those old tin trophies were to him. Biting his lip, Dougie made his way around the bed, sitting at the head end some distance from Mary, placing the cans of pop on to his bedside table.

'Don't worry, mate,' I whispered. 'She doesn't bite. Much.'

Mary closed the remaining distance, bumping up against him. That was all it took to propel Dougie forward off the bed.

'So, I've been reading up on it,' he said to her, crossing to his computer desk and hitting the monitor button.

'What's that?' she asked, a twinge of disappointment in her voice as he sat down in front of his PC.

'Seances,' he replied as the screen pinged into life, revealing a world of internet pages on spooks.

Mary's feet thumped the floor as she crossed the room, coming to a halt behind him. Dougie was immersed in shadows as she leaned forward, her white face appearing across his shoulder. Any hopes that his personal space might remain safe from invasion had been scuttled; the queen of the goths was not giving up so easily.

'You *have* been busy,' she said, clearly impressed.

'You probably know more than any of the clowns I've been speaking to, but there seem to be a few things that are constants. I snaffled some candles from my dad's garage – apparently spirits are drawn to heat and light.' He looked at me. 'Am I right so far?'

'Can't say I've given it much thought, but if it helps then tell her what she needs to hear.'

'You're speaking to him right now?' she asked, once again staring straight through me.

'Course,' Dougie replied. 'Like I said, he's here *all* the time. Right, what else is there . . .' He started scrolling through one of the web pages that had proved especially helpful. Mary continued to glance around the room, at no point registering my existence.

While there was no arguing with her gothic credentials – she certainly looked the part with her clothes, make-up and constantly surly attitude – I was finding it difficult to believe that this girl had any real occult powers. If she was a spiritualist as she claimed to be, then surely she'd have seen me by now, or at the very least acknowledged I was present? As a lifelong disbeliever in anything supernatural – especially so-called mediums – it was hard enough for *me* to believe in ghosts, and I *was* one! I noticed she was now staring at Dougie, her eyes lingering over his still-spiky hair.

She clearly wasn't listening as he rattled on enthusiastically, expounding his theories on what they needed to do in order for her to speak with me. Her eyes were now on the nape of his neck, pale and exposed where his collar was open. Did she just lick her lips? I was beginning to get a bad feeling about this.

'Um . . . Dougie,' I said, but he was utterly in the zone as he imparted his newfound wisdom and paid me no attention.

'Since you never actually met Will, you don't know who you're looking for,' he said, tapping a shoebox beside the keyboard. 'I've got some of his personal artefacts here: school photographs, a couple of CDs he lent me, roleplay dice, a pair of shades I nicked off him in the summer, that kinda thing. I've also turned off my mobile phone – you might want to do the same – as that's just the kind of distraction I'd imagine might screw things up for you. Sorry – this is probably like teaching your granny how to suck eggs, isn't—'

Mary's lips were suddenly on Dougie's neck, her mouth clamped to his flesh. He let loose a yowl, tearing himself free and squirming out of his chair and on to the floor, the vacated seat spinning behind him like an abandoned kiddie's roundabout.

'Did you just *bite* me?' exclaimed Dougie in disbelief, checking that his neck was still intact. I snorted, torn between feelings of sympathy and hilarity as he scrambled clear of Bloody Mary.

'Oh come on, Nosebleed,' she said, stepping closer to him, her voice now light and giggly. 'I thought you were into the vampire stuff?'

'Yeah, on the telly and in a book, not in real life!' he laughed nervously, his face now flushed with colour. He backed on to the bed, his eyes panicked as she sat near him.

'Sorry,' Mary said, her husky voice at its flirty best. It really wasn't working. 'I didn't mean to startle you. Do you want me to take a look at that? See if I've . . . broken the skin . . .'

She leaned forward, her black fingernails reached for his collar. Did she actually think she was a vampire?

Dougie dodged out of her grasp once more. 'There's been a misunderstanding,' he gasped. 'I thought we were here to get you to communicate with Will!'

'Oh give it up, there's no such thing as ghosts!'

'But . . . but I thought you could speak to the dead!' he stammered frantically.

'Give over. Who really believes in any of that nonsense? Stop playing games, Nosebleed. I know why you invited me here tonight,' she whispered, craning closer for a kiss.

'Wait!' he shrieked, making one last desperate bid to avoid

snogging the most feared girl in school. 'I'm not a goth and my name's not Nosebleed! I'm Dougie, I like Dungeons and Dragons, comics, cartoons and Eighties indie! My hair's spiky because it's full of flippin' glue, and using a Sharpie for eyeliner wasn't hardcore – it was good old-fashioned haplessness! I'm really not into vampires!'

Mary glanced each way conspiratorially. 'I'll let you into a couple of secrets: neither am I! My favourite film is *Seven Brides for Seven Brothers* and my iPod's full of Michael Buble.'

The panic was rising on Dougie's face as he realised he was out of his depth, his face drained of colour. A ghost I may have been, but my insides were knotted, my friend's anxiety seemingly crossing over. Whatever discomfort he felt, I was getting it too, coming off him in waves. He seemed paralysed in the presence of Mary, but I wasn't. I could have left him there to his fate, with the older girl having clearly dramatically misread Dougie's signals, but I couldn't do it. He was my best mate. I did what any friend would do. I intervened.

'Come on, Nosebleed,' she whispered, puckering her lips. 'Gimme some sugar.'

I lashed out, striking one of the cans of pop and propelling it through the air. How did I do it? I couldn't tell you, I wasn't even sure I could replicate it. The can exploded as it hit the wall, ring pull rupturing and sending Dandelion and Burdock across the two of them. That wasn't the alarming part though.

A clear viscous gel oozed from the wall where the can had impacted, rolling down the paper in slow, sticky trails. We were all big enough *Ghostbusters* fans to recognise ectoplasm when we saw it.

That was enough for Bloody Mary. She trampled Dougie on her way to the door, crashing out of the bedroom and down the stairs as she fled the Hancock house in quick time. We looked out of his window, watching her go, wailing as she ran down the street, before turning our attention back to the wall and the ghostly goo.

'How—'

'I have *no* idea,' I said, cutting Dougie off. 'Sorry about the wallpaper, pal. That might take some explaining to your old man.'

'Thanks, mate,' he said with a sheepish shrug.

I put my arm around my friend to comfort him, only for it to pass right through.

I cursed. He laughed.

ELEVEN

Live and Learn

'Well, I think it's fair to say that my flirtation with the Dark Side's been a total disaster,' said Dougie, his voice laden with all the gloom a failed goth could muster.

My mum had a well-worn proverb: *If you've nothing nice to say, best say nothing at all.* I was sticking with this at present. Ordinarily, Dougie would've been ripe for the ribbing that only best friends can hand out, but even my wicked sense of humour opted out on this occasion. Don't get me wrong, I was itching to say *something*, but nothing I could've said would have been funnier than how Dougie already looked.

His hair was gone, shorn off that very morning once it had become clear that the PVA glue had been a distinctly bad idea. Bad because he hadn't used PVA after all: the bottle he'd swiped from his dad's garage had actually contained wood glue. His hair had been the least embarrassing problem to resolve, though. A good half-hour had been spent in the bathroom before he left the house, going through roughly five sink-loads of hot, soapy water as he relentlessly scrubbed at his eyelids to no effect. Two perfect black rings encircled his bleary peepers, giving him the fixed expression of a world-weary panda. The pair of sunglasses he'd resorted to only drew more attention, especially with the grey November skies hanging overhead. And the humiliating pièce de résistance was the love bite on his neck. I'd seen this before in school, usually relatively subtle, but Dougie's wasn't subtle in the least. The enormous circular suckered spot made it look like he'd lost a fight with the Kraken.

'Where does this leave us?' I asked, shadowing my friend as he trudged toward school, scuffing his shoes with each miserable step.

'Well, I've got a new chapter to write in my *Rules of Ghosting* handbook, specifically on older girls and the merits of speaking to so-called psychics. Bloody Mary's typical of that lot. Charlatans, all of them, preying on the hopeless and helpless. I believe the expression is "comforting lies for the criminally gullible" where mediums are concerned.'

'Dunno, mate,' I said. 'Try not to be too closed-minded. You may meet the real McCoy one day. After all, your best friend's a ghost, isn't he?'

Dougie grunted and tugged the fur-trimmed snorkel of his parka about his face.

'I'm really not digging the new me. The bald head and sunglasses make me look like Nosferatu's lovechild,' replied Dougie, scratching his smooth scalp beneath the hood.

'I'd have said you were rocking the Uncle Fester look myself, but I won't argue.' Dougie shot me a glare. 'And *now* I'm done. Promise.'

'You do realise this is entirely down to you?'

'Let's not start a peeing contest! I'm the one who's dead!'

'Fair point,' he grumbled. 'I'll give you that. You should be thankful you've got a mate like me who'll do this to himself,' he said, gesturing from his head to his toes. 'There aren't many friends who'd Frankenweenie themselves for their best buddy.'

I burst out laughing, and thankfully Dougie joined me. The mood instantly lifted, my friend wiping a tear from the corner of his eye as he shook his head.

'I am thankful, mate,' I said. 'I appreciate it more than words. At least we've ruled out Bloody Mary as an answer to my problems. I've seen more psychic ability on *Scooby-Doo*.'

'And we still don't know why I'm the only one who can see you,' added Dougie. 'Perhaps the problem *does* lie with me after all.'

'I don't follow.'

'You could be a figment of my fevered imagination. Perhaps my mind's rustled you up as a way of dealing with the loss.'

'Aw, I never realised you loved me so much,' I said, batting my lashes at him.

'Shut your rattle,' he replied, instinctively lashing out and falling straight through my ghostly form, landing in a hedge. 'What about Rev. Singer?' Dougie asked, brushing the leaves and twigs off his parka as he righted himself on the footpath once more. 'D'you think it's worth seeing Stu's dad?'

'Not if you're hoping he can exorcise me, it's not! He's a vicar, what can he really do?'

'I dunno, but he'll know more than us. Where else can we go?'

'What about Lucy Carpenter?'

'No way, mate,' said Dougie. 'Encounters with the opposite sex? Been there, done that. Bloody Mary's put me off that nonsense for life.'

'But the kiss we shared—'

'The kiss you *say* you shared,' he corrected me.

'Isn't it worth at least talking to her?'

'As a last resort, perhaps,' sighed Dougie, 'but I really can't imagine she'll be able to help. At least Rev. Singer's a vicar. If anyone knows what's what, surely it's him? Let's call round to the church at lunch break, see if Stu's old man can help.'

'And then what?'

'I'm out of ideas. I want to get to the bottom of this just as much as you, Will. We're in this together: you might be the one who's dead but you're still here with me, every minute of the day and night. Don't get me wrong, I miss you something awful and it breaks my heart knowing you're a ghost. But this is no way to live, having you follow me around like a shadow. I want to help you move on, mate, for both our sakes. I want to know what the deal is.'

'The deal?'

'Yeah,' he replied, animated now. 'Will you be around for long? Will you just fade away? I know that sounds horrible, but I've got so many questions, like you probably do too. How long does this go on, you haunting me? Who has the answers to something like this? If you've any ideas I'm all ears.'

Dougie stopped and turned when he realised I wasn't with him any more. I was standing beside a pair of wrought-iron gates that were chained and padlocked shut. A yellow warning sign bore the legend *CONDEMNED* in bold black print, the panel fixed to the rusting bars. Beyond, a gravel driveway disappeared into the trees. I was quiet for a moment before answering him.

'There's always the House. I don't know why we didn't think of it sooner.'

Dougie shivered, and it wasn't the cold that had got to him. Red Brook House dated back to the 1800s, once a boarding school before becoming a state school, but that was about as much as any of us knew about its history. One thing everybody in the neighbourhood *did* know, however, was that it was haunted. The fact it was surrounded by skeletal black woodland, its gravel road was overgrown with brambles, and it had a set of monstrous gothic gates only emphasised that point.

'I know why we didn't think of it sooner,' Dougie said. 'Because it's a bloody scary place.'

'Scarier than the graveyard outside your bedroom window?'

'I grew up in sight of those graves, mate. Played among them enough times, fetching back footballs that disappeared over the fence. There was never really anything to be scared of there.'

'Your Hulk underpants would tell a different story.'

'But the House,' he continued, ignoring my jibe, 'that place reeks of bad news. It's got more horror stories than Stephen King.'

He didn't need to further explain what he meant. In our brief lifetimes a number of tragedies had taken place in or near the old red building. There'd been a suicide in the surrounding woods – a bank manager who'd been a bit overzealous with other people's money. And when we were both in primary school, a couple of senior lads had broken into the House one Halloween as a dare. One had apparently fallen from the main staircase and died, while the other now resided in a mental hospital. How much of this was true was hard to say – stories like that get added to over time – but even if they were just spooky folktales, they'd taken on mythical proportions throughout the school.

'Do you believe any of those stories?' I asked.

'Dunno,' Dougie bravely replied. 'But if *anywhere* is haunted, then it has to be the House.'

'Oi oi! Humpty Dumpty!'

We both turned, looking back down the road to where Vinnie Savage and his mates were following us, or more specifically, following Dougie. Vinnie Savage: he was Lucy Carpenter's boyfriend, or had been. I found myself wondering whether he ever got wind of the kiss I'd stolen from her. Either way, it didn't presently matter. That kiss was unconnected to this encounter. This was just Vinnie's regular name-calling, and not for the first time Dougie was the target. That was one thing I didn't miss: the bullying.

It had been Vinnie who had shouted, his gang joining in, shouting other obscenities Dougie's way. With dismay, my friend realised his hood had fallen down when he'd tumbled into the bushes. Grabbing the fur-trimmed flap of green khaki, he tugged it back over his head, covering his bare scalp once more. I sensed Dougie pick up his pace, trying to put some distance between himself and the mob of morons.

'Don't cover it up, baldy!' shouted another of Vinnie's mates.

'Is he running away?' called a third. 'Oi, Egghead! Come back!'

My heart ached for Dougie as he now began to jog, the pursuing pack of idiots laughing and jeering as they gave chase.

'I never tire of this,' I grumbled as my friend decided to run the remaining distance to school.

'You're the lucky one,' he replied breathlessly. 'You're spared it now.'

He was only half right. As Dougie ran through the school gates, I was dragged along by his side, that familiar feeling of being the prey returning, hunted by a bunch of relentless twits. Just as with Bloody Mary, as his heart rate quickened, his fear crossed over to me. The connection was there, our feelings entwined inextricably. If scumbags like this had us both scared, though, then what on earth were we going to be like in the House?

TWELVE

Father and Son

'Good afternoon, boys,' called Rev. Singer with a wave of a gloved hand. 'I hope you've brought enough chips for everyone?'

The garden behind St Mary's church looked like there'd been an explosion in a confetti factory. Tiny petals of every colour of the rainbow littered the grass, remnants from the weekend wedding that Rev. Singer had officiated over. He was a busy man. Until we'd interrupted him, he'd been busy raking the nuisance litter into a giant pile. In addition to being the parish vicar, Rev. Singer was also effectively the caretaker of the church, as well as gardener. As Dougie and I followed Stu across the lawn toward his father, the vicar bit a finger of his gardening glove and gave it a tug, shaking it loose. He whipped the other free and shoved them in the loop of belt on his hip. Downing his tool he stepped over to us, snatching the can of cola from Stu's coat pocket.

'Good of you to bring refreshments as well as tuck,' he said, ruffling Stu's mop of hair. He picked up a handful of steaming chips as his son shambled past.

'If it isn't young Master Hancock?' said Rev. Singer, his perfect white smile dazzling as Dougie approached sheepishly. He popped a chip in and wolfed it down. 'How are you doing, Dougie? You're looking a bit ... peaky.'

The vicar wasn't wrong. My mate's pale bald head and dark-rimmed eyes did his looks no favour.

'I, um ... have a part in the school play ...' he lied.

'You look like you've seen a ghost,' said Rev. Singer with a wink.

'Did you tell him already?' asked an alarmed Dougie, calling to Stu who had shambled off to a bench to eat his chips. Stu simply shrugged, his mouth full of salt-and-vinegar-drenched potato.

'Tell me what already?' asked Rev. Singer, his smile slipping.

I'd always liked the reverend. It was no surprise that Mum and Dad had asked for him to oversee my funeral. It had been Rev. Singer who had christened me after all, only right he should be looking after me at the end. All of Stu's friends knew he was a friendly ear, someone they could turn to if they were feeling low. He had always been straight with us, never spoke down to us. He was a top bloke.

'Sit yourself down, Dougie,' said the vicar, parking his bottom on a nearby bench. Dougie went to join him. 'Tell me what's the matter, my boy.'

My friend shifted nervously on the wooden seat, trying to think of where to begin.

'Tell him you've seen me,' I whispered, simply. Dougie glanced up at me, and Rev. Singer saw the look.

'Has this got something to do with Will Underwood?

Dougie did a double-take instantly, eyes wide as he stared suspiciously at the vicar. 'You *did* say something!' he shouted to Stu.

'I said nowt,' replied our friend, his mouth full of chips. 'My old man's a bit of a wizard when it comes to sniffing out the truth. It's like he's telepathic!'

Rev. Singer shook his head and smiled. 'Empathetic is the word you're searching for, Stuart,' he sighed. 'I like to think I understand what makes folk unhappy. Hopefully I can play my part to make that sadness go away.'

I didn't like his choice of words. *Go away?* That could only mean one thing.

'For goodness' sake,' I said. 'Don't ask him to exorcise me!'

'I've seen nothing of you since Will's funeral, Dougie, and I know you and he were very close. Grief is nothing to be ashamed of, my boy. If you're upset, why don't you try talking about it? I'm a good listener. Isn't that right, Stuart?'

'Painfully good!' replied his son, slurping vinegar from his fingers.

'People deal with grief and loss in different ways, Dougie,' the vicar went on. 'I can only speak from my own experience, but I've always felt that talking to friends and loved ones is a start. If you want to have a cry, then have a good cry. There's nothing to fear from tears.'

Dougie sniffed and fought back a sobbing chuckle. I felt my friend's sadness, the mixed emotions that had clearly weighed heavy upon his shoulders since the night I'd died. And the days that had followed, when I'd reappeared. He wasn't grieving: how could he? I hadn't gone away!

'What's your take on ghosts, Rev. Singer?' he asked eventually, looking up to stare into the vicar's eyes.

Stu's dad looked taken aback momentarily. He nodded.

'I firmly believe most "hauntings" are no more supernatural than that bag of chips my son is devouring.' Stu snorted as his father continued. 'They're a manifestation of an internalised fear or vulnerability. Strange sounds, weird happenings, inexplicable phenomena and the like: people conjure ghost theories to help explain these things when there's usually a rational explanation. This is how they deal with the real fear.'

'But what about if we've actually *seen* something, sir?' said Dougie. 'Something that can't be written off so easily. Something that defies rational explanation?'

'It's perfectly normal for us to imagine our loved ones are still with us, spiritually, even when they're physically gone.'

'He said *loved ones*,' I whispered, but Dougie wisely ignored me.

'It's terribly hard for us to accept that those we love are gone, especially when they're taken from us in such a sudden and shocking fashion. Will's death took us all by surprise, being completely unexpected. Nobody, be they friends or family, got a chance to say goodbye to him. As such, the pain can be that much greater.'

The vicar sighed once more.

'You think you've seen Will's ghost?' he asked. Dougie didn't answer straight away, so Rev. Singer continued.

'Regret is a terrible thing. Perhaps this is how that "ghostly presence" manifests? Maybe it's born out of a sensation of guilt, of unfinished business. Imagining those loved ones are still with us is our subconscious's way of dealing with that loss. These are powerful emotions we're talking about, Dougie. It's perfectly normal for you to think you've seen Will. Seen ... a ghost.'

'But you're a vicar,' said Dougie. 'Surely you believe in *actual* ghosts? There was a holy one for starters, wasn't there?'

Stu snorted nearby and even Rev. Singer smiled at Dougie's mild and unintentional blasphemy.

'Actual ghosts?' said Rev. Singer. 'Apparitions and whatnot? The church has its own take on that too. We do believe in a spirit world. And even amongst the clergy there are different interpretations. Like anything in life – and death – opinions vary.'

'So what are your opinions on ghosts?' asked Dougie. 'And I'm not talking about the grief or sorrow of the living, Rev. Singer.'

I leaned in close, crouching before the two of them, the church garden silent but for the chip-chomping din of the vicar's son.

'When I studied theology at university, back in the day, a friend of mine was something of a budding ghosthunter,' said Rev. Singer.

'Like in *Ghostbusters*?' chimed in Stu.

'Not quite, son,' smiled Rev. Singer before continuing. 'He had his theories, as I recall. He reckoned there were probably two kinds of ghost that haunt the living world. There's your restless spirit, born from a sudden and tragic death.'

'Like a murder?'

'Not always a murder, Dougie, but sometimes a terrible trauma or mishap. One can be guaranteed that some kind of injustice is involved, though. Most reported ghosts the length and breadth of the British Isles would fall into this category in my opinion: White Ladies sighted, residual recordings of strange sounds, haunted houses and the like. These poor souls, often due to trauma, are stuck in our physical world and need to be released before they can go on.'

If there'd been any moisture in my mouth, my lips would have been dry about now. I saw Dougie shiver as Rev. Singer paused, his brow furrowing.

'The other kind? Well ... my friend said that would be a malevolent spirit, the ghost of a bad man or woman. And that would place us firmly into the realm of an exorcist. I can bless a troubled soul or place, but dealing with such an entity would be beyond the realms of a lay priest or vicar's knowledge.'

'Bear in mind I'm in the *former* camp,' I said, 'so I think we can rule out the exorcism.'

'What would you do in those circumstances?' asked Dougie, his enquiring mind now begging the question.

We both stared at Rev. Singer as he considered his answer.

'I'd defer matters to my seniors within the church,' he said eventually, popping the last chip into his mouth. 'But I should say, Dougie, all this talk of exorcism is highly alarmist.'

Rev. Singer rose and stretched, looking around the church garden. He turned back to Dougie who was frowning, contemplating the vicar's words.

'Listen, Dougie, try not to worry. I have a youth group that gets together once a week, where teens can talk about anything that's bothering them amongst their peers. We deal with a lot of issues there. Nothing heavy-handed from the grown-ups, yeah? You could come along to that. Share your thoughts. I bet our Stuart would come along too for a bit of moral support. Isn't that right, son?'

Stu grunted as he scrumpled up his chip papers and slam-dunked them into a litter bin. Dougie rose from the bench as the vicar's son joined him, swiping the can of cola back from his dad.

'Thanks for your time, Rev. Singer,' said Dougie. 'I'll think about that youth group,' he lied.

'Tell your dad I run a group for adults too. It'd be lovely to see him down here, if he fancies it.'

'See you later, Dad,' said Stu, giving his father a quick hug before setting off after Dougie.

'Why should your dad need to go to one of the talks?' I asked, glancing back at the vicar as he returned to work.

'He suffers,' replied Dougie quietly, keeping his voice low as Stu caught up.

He wasn't wrong. Mr Hancock had been ill with depression since he lost his wife. His driving job certainly didn't appear to make him happy, and his son was always worried about him. Not many people knew about it, and it wasn't something Dougie advertised. It just went to show how on-the-ball Rev. Singer was. Dougie and his dad may not have been to church for years, but there was little that went on amongst his parishioners that the vicar was unaware of.

'You get what you need then?' asked Stu, cracking open his can of cola and taking a glug.

'I think we've finally ruled out exorcism,' conceded Dougie, 'which just leaves us with one thing left to explore.'

'What's that then?' said Stu, stifling a hearty belch as we set off back to school.

'The House,' I whispered, my friend and I shivering as one.

'The House,' added Dougie as storm clouds gathered overhead, right on cue.

'The House?' said Stu. 'Good luck with that! You're on your own!'

'Don't worry, mate,' I said in Dougie's ear. 'We both know that's not true.'

THIRTEEN

Breaking and Entering

'Just suck your gut in and squeeze through!'

'That's easy for you to say,' hissed Dougie as he tried to manoeuvre between the chained gates. 'You're as free to float through as a fart on the breeze!'

Pushing the gates to their limit, the length of steel links straining taut, Dougie ducked beneath it, his right leg and shoulder dipping through.

'You could always try and jump the railings,' I said constructively, staring up at the fierce-looking wrought-iron spears that encircled the grounds' perimeter.

'No thanks,' replied my friend, forcing his head between the grilled doors. 'I'm rather attached to my undercarriage.'

With a final triumphant grunt his head popped through the gates, quickly followed by the rest of his body as he collapsed on to the gravel driveway beyond. I stepped through after him, the iron bars providing no obstacle to my insubstantial form. It was past four o'clock, with the late November gloom providing us with cover as we embarked upon our daring mission. Within the House was the solution to our riddle. If those legends we'd grown up on were even slightly true, then something in there would provide us with answers. Hunting a ghost might have struck us both as outlandish not that long ago, but times changed. After all, I was one now. Surely I wasn't alone? We were both agreed that somehow the House would shed some light on the fate that had befallen us.

Dougie set off at a jog, hugging the centre of the weed-ridden driveway, steering clear of the tangled undergrowth on either side of the road. Ahead, the red-brick monstrosity loomed large out of the twilight, a mausoleum to a time long gone, the surrounding woodland buttressing up against it. Bare black branches clawed at the House in the wind, scratching at the pitted, vine-covered walls. Two huge doors marked the entrance to the building, towering menacingly at the top of a flight of shattered stone steps. Broken windows yawned open, their shutters hanging twisted from their brackets, the occasional *kaw* of a crow echoing from deep within. This was the closest either of us had ever been to the structure, and instantly I felt a desire to be away from it. Dougie obviously felt the same way, as he stumbled to a halt, his legs having failed him.

'Easy, mate,' I said as he staggered off the road to crouch beside a tangle of brambles and hawthorns. 'Just take a few breaths.'

'It's not just me, is it?' he asked. 'You're creeped out too, right?'

I smiled nervously, but he'd hit the nail right on the head. 'I know. What the hell? I'm a ghost: what have I got to be afraid of?'

Dougie took a deep breath and was about to set off the remaining distance to the house when, 'Down,' I hissed, and the two of us – boy and ghost – instantly crouched back into the bushes.

'What is it?' he whispered, his eyes following my gaze toward the front of the House.

One of the enormous doors had opened, and a crooked shape had emerged from the shadows within. The bent-backed figure was now fiddling with the locks. Even from our distant hiding place we could hear the mechanism rattle as the stranger secured the entrance. Shuffling clear of the darkened threshold, the man stepped into the fading light.

'It's Mr Borley!' gasped Dougie, the words out in an instant. He clapped his hand over his mouth, but the old school caretaker had already stopped on the steps and was glancing about in our direction. He squinted through the gloom, giving the grounds a quick once-over, before setting off down the steps and along the gravel road. We watched him pass by from our hiding place, shrouded in shadows, Dougie holding his breath like a bottled genie. The rattling sound of the chains at the gate told us that Borley had finally departed. Dougie slowly exhaled.

'What was he doing here?' he asked. 'And how come he has the keys to the House?'

'Dunno,' I replied. 'It used to be part of the school, right? Perhaps as caretaker he's got keys to everything, old and new?'

Dougie set off across the gravel forecourt. 'Let's see what he's been hiding in here. I always said he was a creepy old git.'

'Forget Borley,' I hissed. 'It's the dead we've come looking for, remember?'

I drifted after my friend, up the crumbling steps toward the doors. As Dougie pointlessly tried the clunking handles, I stepped forward, slipping with ease through the timber and into the House. The moon's rays were already arcing in through the shattered windows, lances of light cutting through the cold, dusty air to the debris-strewn floor. A broad, sweeping staircase rose up one side of the entrance hall, meeting a landing on the first floor before rising to the second. An ancient chandelier hung from the ceiling at the staircase's height, fluttering cobwebs trailing from its rusted limbs. I'd never seen a chandelier in a school before: Brooklands Comp tended to favour flickering strip lighting that could induce epileptic seizures. Red Brook House, however, had once been a swanky private school long ago, before becoming a state school. The fancy fixture was clearly a relic of those days.

My feet hovered over the rotten floorboards as I crossed the entrance hall to the wall at the base of the staircase. Large, wooden frames were fixed to the plasterboard, bearing the faded names of head boys and girls from yesteryear. The last date inscribed told the tale of the school's closure: 1966.

I turned, casting my eyes about, soaking in the atmosphere. More than any other time since my untimely death, I felt alive. I know it sounds weird – but I could *imagine* the smells in the entrance hall, the musty stench of damp and mould, birds' nests and bat guano. I might never feel the cold again, but the House was as close as I'd ever come to experiencing it one more time. Every inch of the red-brick building was soaked in history, the names on the wall alone conjured images of a time long gone, when the old school echoed with the sound of laughter, running feet, shouting children and slamming doors. I closed my eyes, imagining that world, frozen in time.

'Cheers, numbnuts!'

Dougie's voice startled me, coming out of nowhere, right in my ear.

'Look at me, making a ghost jump,' he chuckled, dusting himself down. 'Thanks for waiting,' he added sarcastically, eyes wide as they searched the darkness.

'How did you get in?'

'Ground-floor window,' he said, nodding towards a side room that branched off from the hall. 'This place is huge inside!'

'I know. Imagine what it was like in the old days. Must've really been something. If these walls could talk . . .'

'They'd recount the various terrible things that have happened here down the years,' finished Dougie. 'Remember why we're here, Will. This place has apparently seen more hauntings than Derek Acorah.'

'Do you really believe that?' I said, stepping up to the base of the stairs and passing my hand through the polished curved banister. 'I mean, now that we're here? Look at the place, Dougie. Yes, it's old, dusty and creaky, but so is my nan and she ain't scary.'

'I beg to differ,' said Dougie, stepping after me and staying close. 'Your nan tried to kiss me last Christmas under the mistletoe.'

'You tried to kiss her, you mean.'

'That's right,' answered Dougie. 'Snogging grannies is just my bag, mate. She still doesn't return my calls.'

'I think she's been scared off by Bloody Mary,' I sniggered.

'It must be hard for the old dear to compete with talent like that.'

'Putting Mary to one side for a moment – about a hundred miles to one side – what are you trying to say? You don't think the House is haunted now?'

'What I'm saying is, I don't think there's anything really scary here. An old building like this always gets singled out for ghost stories, and it does look pretty Addams Family on the surface, but I reckon when you blow the dust and cobwebs away, it's just a piece of history.'

'We've got the wrong end of the stick, mate,' I went on with a shrug. 'There's only one ghost here, and you're looking at him.'

Dougie sat down on the bottom step, hunching his shoulders as he rubbed his hands together.

'So why was Borley here?'

'I've absolutely *no* idea,' I replied. 'We're looking for ghosts. What's Borley's excuse?'

'It's arctic in here,' Dougie said, his breath now steaming before his face. He reached up and grabbed the banister, about to haul himself up.

'Bloody hell!' he shouted, crying out as his hand remained fixed to the polished wood.

'What's the matter?'

I watched as my friend struggled to remove his hand from

the rail. I could see his skin clinging to the surface, frost spreading across the banister in a wave of tiny white crystals. He tried to pry his fingers loose with his free hand, his teeth chattering as he spoke.

'My hand's stuck! The wood's f-f-freezing!'

'What? How can that be?'

Dougie's breath was billowing and clouding around him now as if he were on fire. Even I felt it – heaven knows how – the temperature drop striking at my own cold dead heart. Dougie's eyes were wide suddenly as he stared up the staircase toward the first-floor landing. It was my turn to follow his gaze.

She was probably a touch younger than us, maybe Year Seven, pale blonde hair tied into pigtails with red ribbons. I didn't recognise her uniform, a drab grey pinafore and tights with a threadbare cardigan over the top. Her head was dipped, chin resting upon her chest so her face was obscured.

'Who are you?' I said to her. 'Why are you here?'

Dougie whimpered beside me, slowly prising his fingers away from the frozen wooden rail. He was gasping with cold. I knew he couldn't survive in this temperature more than a few minutes.

The girl's head rose suddenly, revealing her pale face. Her eyes were closed, as if she were sleepwalking. She swayed ever so slightly. I advanced up the staircase, my ghostly feet brushing the steps.

'Be careful!' I called to her.

The girl's eyes flew open. Twin pools of black stared out at us, voids of terrible darkness that grew as Dougie and I watched in horror. Like Munch's painting, her jaw yawned open to monstrous proportions, as screams of our own escaped our lips. A banshee wail washed over the pair of us in a sickening wave.

I turned, rushing through the petrified Dougie and stirring him into action. He ripped his hand free from the banister and ran through the debris of the hall, dashing for the window he'd entered by. I was there, waiting for him, beyond the walls of the red-brick building as my friend came tumbling through the splintered window frame. He landed in some brambles and scrambled up, still gibbering with cold as the girl's ghostly cry sent us on our way. I glanced back just the once, as the dark red House at our back was swallowed up by the gathering night.

FOURTEEN

Shaken and Stirred

'Well?' I said. 'What the hell happened back there?'

We were back in Dougie's house, safely ensconced in the bathroom. Beside me, Dougie gargled and spat, a glob of foamy toothpaste hitting the sink. 'We saw a ghost! Scratch that, *another* flipping ghost! A scary one this time.'

'What's that, son?' shouted Mr Hancock from downstairs, a hint of concern in his voice.

'Nothing, Dad. Just er ... talking to myself,' he called out.

'Great,' muttered Dougie. 'Now Dad'll think I'm insane. The day just gets better.'

He popped his toothbrush into the pot and stared into the bathroom mirror. The bleary, black-ringed eyes glared back, his shaven head shiny under the ceiling spotlights.

'Look at the state of me,' he sighed.

'You look like death, and I should know,' I replied. 'Sorry. Couldn't help it.'

'I set 'em up, you knock 'em in,' he said, turning and stepping through the bathroom doorway. The fact that I was filling the space caused him no concern, my best mate walked through me as if I wasn't even there, then stomped off to his bedroom.

'That's still really rude,' I said, shivering before following behind him. There might not have been a physical sensation when anything passed through my ghostly form, but it was still impossible to get used to.

'Anyway, what happened to you saying there weren't any spooks there apart from you?'

'So I get things wrong occasionally,' I shrugged sheepishly. In that moment it was clear I'd still an awful lot to learn about being a ghost. Perhaps I was too connected to the world of the living?

'That was the freakiest thing I've ever laid eyes on,' said Dougie, 'and bear in mind I've seen you in the knack at the swimming baths.'

'I wonder who she was, how she came to be there,' I whispered as Dougie collapsed on to his bed. 'There's probably a record of her death somewhere. Someone must know.'

'All I know is she's gotta be bad news,' he replied, shivering as he stared up at the ceiling. 'Her face. God, I've never seen anything like that before. Never want to again. The face-melting spectres at the end of *Raiders of the Lost Ark* made me pee my pants when I was eight, but they were nothing compared to her.'

'I felt it too,' I said. 'I might not have a body, but I felt the fear as sure as you did.'

I thought again about that terrible face, contorting and twisting out of shape as her scream sent us running. The horror had been all too real to us, but there was more to it than that. I was missing something, I was sure of it.

'Perhaps it's *her* fear we're feeling, rather than our own?'

Dougie shook his head. 'That felt like my fear all right.'

'Maybe it was transference? I've noticed that when you get anxious or frightened, so do I. It happened at the House, and before then too, when Vinnie Savage and his mates were taunting you. I can't explain it but we've some sort of connection. Just as your feelings seem to cross over to me, perhaps we were somehow picking up on hers? Maybe she was just lonely, or miserable? Perhaps she was as afraid of us as we were of her?'

'Mate, she was dishing out the fear,' Dougie said. 'I didn't feel sorry for her. I was scared of her. Still am, for that matter.'

'We need to go back.'

'Are you on crazy pills or what?' he exclaimed, sitting bolt upright in bed. 'There's no way on earth I'm returning to Red Brook House now. Not after that.'

'But we need to try and speak with her. She might be able to help. Can't you see that?'

'You want to know what I see? I see her finishing the job if we go back there.'

'Finishing the job?'

Dougie raised a hand, revealing the frost-burned flesh that marked his palm. 'I've left a good few layers of skin on that banister. The unnatural cold, the sickening screams; who knows what other tricks she's got up her sleeve? Who's to say she won't try and kill me if I go back?'

'You're just being stupid now.'

'Easy for you to say, you've nothing to be afraid of: you're already dead!'

'I *felt* the same fear as you, Dougie. You, me, her – there was a connection of some kind, I'm sure of it. She didn't want you dead. She just wanted you out of there, I reckon.'

'All the more reason why we don't return then,' he said, collapsing back into his pillow. 'She made a very convincing argument. I'm sold.'

'But she might have answers,' I snarled, getting angry now. 'If I can just speak to her, try and reason with her, show her we're no threat—'

'I ain't going back,' said Dougie, shaking his head, arms folded.

'Then I'll go alone.'

'Good luck with that. You're unable to leave me, aren't you?'

'It's my only chance to find out what's going on with this ghost lark. Please, Dougie ...'

'No! It's not all about you, you know. I'm not going, so stop pestering me!'

My temper finally got the better of me in the face of Dougie's stubborn responses. I lashed my pale, ghostly fist out, punching at thin air, letting out my pent-up frustration. The anglepoise on Dougie's bedside table suddenly spun around in its housing. The lamp head struck the wall and the bulb shattered. Once again, a smear of goo oozed from the point of impact, trickling in globs down the wallpaper.

'What. The. Hell?' Even by the dim light of the landing I could see that Dougie's eyes were wide like saucers. 'Again with the vandalising my bedroom! I'll have nothing left of my allowance at this rate. How do you do that?'

'I didn't do anything!' I gasped, scared by my own power. 'You must've knocked it that time!'

'With my arms folded? I suppose that's my ectoplasm too?'

I stared at my trembling hands and back to the broken lamp. How could I have done that? That was the second time

I'd properly connected with something solid in the real world. Was it connected to my emotions?

'Will,' said Dougie quietly, 'I can't do this. I'm not going back to the House. Not after what happened. I can handle you. You're my mate. But what we saw back there . . . I'm not ready to face that again. I'd do anything else, but not that.'

'What about Borley?' I whispered. 'Isn't that worth investigating?' I was desperately racking my brains for reasons why Dougie should go back – and Borley seemed a good starting point. Dougie had always loved a good mystery.

'Maybe. One day.' He shrugged. 'Dunno. But the way I feel right now . . . One ghost in my life is more than enough. You might think she isn't dangerous, but not all ghosts are good guys like you.'

'But—'

'No buts,' he said, raising his scarred hand to silence me. 'Monstrous phantoms and hit-and-runs – it all scares me something stupid, Will. It's my life on the line now, and if we're going to find out why you're trapped here, I suggest we start looking in the light instead of searching the dark places.'

'Looking in the light?'

'That unfinished business you said you had? Remember?'

'What are you getting at?'

'Perhaps we've been searching for answers in the wrong place. We've been chasing ghosts and killer cars when perhaps the truth lies closer to home. Perhaps it *is* love that's keeping you here.'

I managed to smile, my dark mood lifting as I thought back to that fleeting moment of happiness on the night of my death. Closing my eyes, I could still taste her kiss, if I concentrated really hard.

'Lucy Carpenter,' I said. 'I thought you didn't believe me?'

'Perhaps she does hold the key after all,' he said with a grin. 'If I can speak with her, put you in touch with each other, maybe then you can move on?'

'And how do you do that?'

'It won't be easy,' replied Dougie. 'I'm not in her class for anything, and her spare time's taken up with hockey and dance. I need to get close to her.'

'I've seen you dance: it looks like you're having a fit. You any good at hockey?'

He fell back on to the duvet and sighed. 'I guess we're going to find out.'

101

FIFTEEN

Hide and Seek

They say you never forget your first kiss. Mine was cherry-flavoured – lip balm to be precise. In a matter of moments my favourite flavour in the world had shifted from Chunky Kit-Kat to cherry and I'd felt no remorse. The chocolate had had a good run, it couldn't complain. Let the little kids have the brown stuff; I'd moved on.

I know what you're thinking: fifteen years old and this is his first kiss? I'd love to tell you that I was saving myself for Miss Right to come flouncing round the corner, but who am I kidding? I'd always been painfully shy around the fairer sex. Acne and a tinge of ginge in my hair didn't do much for my self-esteem. My comfort zone was based predominantly around making girls laugh, a bit of cheeky banter ensuring I was noticed in the crowd. But the moment a friendship had the potential to move on to something bigger that involved sweaty palms, racing heartbeats and gut-wrenching bouts of nausea, I'd retreat into myself. It's safe to say that up until that cherry kiss I was pretty much girlphobic.

I'd had a crush on Lucy Carpenter since I'd started high school. I don't think I'll ever forget seeing her on our first induction day: dark hair, green eyes and a beguiling smile that whispered of mischief. She was clever too, top set just like me and, for whatever reason – possibly a head trauma – she liked me. Not as boyfriend material, you understand, but I made her giggle. We wrote messages to one another during classes in the backs of our homework diaries. She always had boyfriends: big lads, the kind who sauntered out of the school gate for sly smokes at break time. I was never going to get a look-in, so I never tried. I was happy just to get a laugh from her. Never in a million years did I ever imagine I'd steal a kiss.

Her boyfriend, Vinnie Savage, was out of the picture, having been dumped the previous week. She and I had found ourselves alone in a dark corner of the precinct that fateful night. And she had kissed me. Lucy bloody Carpenter had *kissed* me! No words had been spoken, no feelings exchanged – her friends had hollered, calling her back to the pack. I'd been left to fumble my way into my bike saddle and set off on my way, to Dougie's house. To tell him my news. Only, as we well know, I never got there . . .

Loitering around the hockey pitch hadn't been our first plan of action when it came to catching Lucy's eye. We'd resorted to this after all else had failed. The ever charming Vinnie Savage was firmly back on the scene and in Lucy's life. He was a hulking shadow, following her wherever she went. That made normal approaches to catch her attention nigh on impossible. For whatever reason, Savage had taken a particular dislike to my buddy. Seeing Lucy, one on one, was proving a decidedly tricky challenge for my chum.

Initial attempts to catch Lucy's attention had involved Dougie hanging around the dance studio as the girls filed in and out. This had been short-lived, with the fierce Miss Roberts, the head of girls' PE, chasing him off. Putting his name down for the hockey team try-outs hadn't been such a good idea either. Nobody had mentioned to Dougie that the hockey team was girls only, and when he appeared one lunch hour for the trials – the sole boy in a sea of girls – it was yet again Miss Roberts who sent him away. Shamefaced, he'd sloped off, deciding to choose a different approach for attracting Lucy's attention.

'You know, of all your ideas, this looks the worst by some distance,' I said as Dougie shuffled through the bushes beside

104

the hockey field. A steady stream of short-skirted girls filed out of the sports block, spreading out on to the pitch, drawing ever nearer. In the week since our nerve-shredding visit to the House, Dougie's eye make-up had faded and his hair had started growing back, making him now look less Humpty Dumpty and more like Action Man. Still, I didn't reckon it would end well should any of the girls spy him in the bushes. Of the girl in the House, little had been said, but her existence hung over the pair of us like a dark, brooding shadow.

'I didn't see you coming up with any better plans,' Dougie scowled. 'She's always got someone with her. If it's not Vinnie and his pack sniffing about then it's her girlfriends. She's never alone!'

'She isn't alone here, either,' I replied. 'If you hadn't noticed, she's playing in a hockey team.'

'Ah, but she's a *winger*, isn't she? She'll be up and down the touchline, so I can grab her for a chat.'

'Mate, you shouldn't even be here. If Miss Roberts catches you after the other incidents, she'll have you in front of Goodman before you know it. She already thinks you're a pervert.'

'Hush,' he said with a wave of the hand. 'Here she comes.'

And there she was, walking towards us, her best mate Annabel Groves at her side. Each of them carried a hockey stick, and both wore the distinctive school games kit. The girls' giggles were interrupted as Dougie suddenly stood upright, the bushes parting around him. Annabel shrieked as Lucy stopped in her tracks, both of them hoisting their sticks defensively.

'Um . . . hello!' said Dougie, rocking from one foot to the other, his hands buried in his trouser pockets. He'd never been good at talking with girls, often turning into a bag of nerves in their presence. Bloody Mary had provided her own challenges, being an older and far more intimidating presence, but Dougie had just played a character there. The hapless 'Nosebleed' wasn't one of his finest creations. This encounter looked decidedly trickier: he had nowhere to hide, no mask to hide behind. He had to be himself. With Lucy, an undisputed beauty, his go-to approach usually involved talking gibberish or breathtaking silence. It was all or nothing with Dougie.

Annabel glared at him before turning to her friend. 'Miss Roberts said we were to tell her if he turned up again. He's one of them Peeping Toms – you're not really going to speak to him, are you?'

'It's about Will,' Dougie yelped, his final gambit coming out as a high-pitched squeak. I watched as Lucy's face softened, her eyebrows arching sympathetically.

'What about Will?' she said, lowering her hockey stick.

Annabel rolled her eyes and huffed dramatically before marching away back toward the other girls in the centre of the playing field.

'She really doesn't like me, does she?' Dougie said, peering around Lucy as he watched her friend flounce off.

Lucy cleared her throat with a cough, drawing Dougie's eyes back to her. 'Will, Dougie? What about him?'

'This might sound a bit weird . . .' he began, struggling to find the words.

'What? It gets weirder than you stalking me for a week?'

'That's a bit unfair, isn't it?'

'She's got a point,' I interjected. 'You have just leaped out of some bushes at her.'

'Shut up, you,' he said, turning to me.

Lucy flinched. 'OK . . . just got weirder. Who are you talking to?'

He raised his palms up before him as he took a step toward her. 'You're going to think I've got a screw loose so please bear with me.'

'Quickly shifting from weird to scary, Dougie,' I said. 'If you're going to say something say it now!'

'You see . . . Will – he hasn't gone away.'

Lucy frowned suspiciously. 'Dougie, you were there with me at the funeral home. It was a cremation, remember? Will's gone.'

'No,' said Dougie earnestly, wringing his hands now. 'He's still here.'

Now Lucy dipped her head to one side and smiled sadly, her voice heavy with sympathy as she stepped up to him.

'I've heard about this kind of thing, Dougie. And I get it, I really do. You don't want to admit Will's gone, you can't accept he's no longer with us. So your mind will make up anything to ease that loss. Is that what the shaved head and the black eyes are all about? A cry for help? Makes sense now.'

Dougie shook his head. 'No, it's not that. There's no easy way of putting this, so I'm just gonna come out and say it.' He took a breath. 'Will's a ghost.'

'He's a what?'

'A spook, a phantom.'

'You realise how mad you sound?'

'I'm telling you the truth!'

'You're telling me he's back from the dead, like some kind of zombie?'

'Not a zombie, no, that'd be awful, shambling around, bits falling off him, stinking the place up. No, he's your common or garden ghost, a regular wispy, smoking spectre. He's here right now, just beside us.'

Naturally she turned the wrong way and not towards me. Dougie whistled and nodded his head in my direction. She stared right through me, searching the air for a telltale sign. Suddenly she shook her head and gave him a shove.

'This is ridiculous,' she said with annoyance, threatening him with her hockey stick again. 'You had me for a moment there. What sort of sick game are you playing?'

'It's no game! He hasn't been able to move on, he's stuck here in limbo. And what's worse, he's following me everywhere I go.'

'That's bad, is it?' I exclaimed.

'Yes it is bad, numpty!'

'I take it that was for Will's benefit?' she said sarcastically.

'Of course it was!' said Dougie, losing his rag at last. 'The reason I've been stalking you – as you so kindly put it – is because I wanted to put you in touch with him. He's my best mate and I figure the two of you might have some unfinished business!'

'What unfinished business?' she asked, bemused.

Dougie turned and looked straight at me. 'You'd better be telling me the truth, dude, or I'm going to look like such a pillock . . .'

'What truth?' said Lucy, looking more than a little worried as Dougie spoke to thin air.

'You know,' he said, making big eyes my way as if he suddenly couldn't speak in front of me.

'No I don't, hence the question,' she said with annoyance.

'*The kiss*,' he said out of the corner of his mouth with all the conspiratorial guile of a pantomime villain.

'Well disguised,' I said, clapping my hands in a mocking fashion. 'Didn't catch a word of that.'

'The kiss?' she said incredulously. 'On the night he died? It was nice, but we were just friends. It was no big deal.'

'Why would she say that?' I yelped at Dougie.

Dougie waved me away. 'It really meant nothing to you?'

'Sorry,' she said, her face now reddening as behind her the other girls were gathering. Annabel was pointing our way, Miss Roberts having now materialised in their midst.

I turned my back on her and faced my friend. I knew I was invisible to her, that she couldn't see me if she tried, but I didn't want to show her just how gutted I was.

'I've heard enough. Can we go, please?'

'Just a minute,' Dougie said, lifting his hand to silence me as he glowered at her. 'Is this how you get your kicks, leading lads on? Will thought you really liked him.'

'Hancock!' shouted Miss Roberts as she began to march towards the touchline, the girls streaming behind her. 'Come here, you horrible boy!'

That was enough for Dougie. Self-preservation kicked in and he was off, bounding back into the bushes as he headed away from the playing field, Miss Roberts in hot pursuit, wielding a hockey stick menacingly.

SIXTEEN

Knock and Run

In the aftermath of the hockey field fiasco, I realised it was time to start retracing my steps, see if I'd missed something in the search for ghostly answers. Where better to begin than back within the four familiar walls of my family home, close to Mum and Dad? I hadn't returned since I'd first drifted off to Dougie's after the funeral. The connection I'd found in my friend's company had been missing at home, my parents and brother in their own little worlds, but perhaps I'd find what I was looking for now. The reason I was stuck here in the land of the living remained a puzzle. Might my parents hold the key? I hoped so, given Lucy had totally failed me.

'Not being funny, mate, but you're better off dead than worrying about impressing Lucy Carpenter,' Dougie said as we approached my front door.

'Really?' I said incredulously as we came to my front porch. 'You're going with that expression?'

'Oh right,' he said sheepishly.

'I'll see you in there,' I said, shifting through the closed uPVC door as Dougie hit the doorbell. Across the threshold, a charge of electricity raced up and down my spine. Though this was the house I'd grown up in, it felt both familiar and odd at the same time. I'd left my family behind to seek out Dougie after my death, so I felt like an intruder in my own home now, and it was an uneasy sensation.

My mum came striding through the living room, causing me to instinctively step to one side to allow her to pass. My heart soared to see her, but another feeling hit me: guilt. Had it been selfish of me to rush off to be with my best friend? Should I have stayed close to her, witnessed her mourning first-hand? Was this my punishment? A quick glance at Mum told me worrying was unnecessary. She was smiling as she opened the door.

'Douglas, love, how are you?' she exclaimed, reaching out and wrapping him up in a maternal hug. 'Come in, come in!' My mate was on tiptoes in an instant as he was dragged, teetering, through the porch and into the house.

'Who is it?' came another voice from the back of the house, as a second woman appeared. Shorter, and altogether more spherical than my mum, it was Val, our next-door neighbour. She was always round when I was alive and nothing had changed since my death by the look of things. Bizarrely, both of them were wearing tracksuits.

'Watch out for Val,' I warned. 'She's loud, bubbly and prone to inappropriate hugging!'

'It's young Douglas, our Will's friend,' replied Mum, propelling him into the room. 'You remember him, don't you? What are you doing here, lovely?'

'Keep moving, mate,' I said as Val made to give him a hug of her own. He deftly side-stepped her and kept a clear line of sight for the front door.

'I felt I ought to pop by and say hello,' replied Dougie. 'I didn't get a chance to speak to you at . . . at the funeral.'

'Oh bless you, young man,' said Val. 'You're a thoughtful one, aren't you, dear?'

'Ask Mum where Dad is,' I whispered into his ear.

'Where's Mr Underwood?'

'He's working out in the gym,' said Mum, gesticulating toward the staircase.

'I didn't know you had one.'

'We didn't used to,' she replied sheepishly. 'It's just now that we've got the box room back we've done a spot of decorating. He's on the rowing machine at present.'

'*Got the box room back?*' I hissed in Dougie's ear, causing him to flinch. 'What was I? Some unwanted lodger or what? That was my bedroom!'

'The gym was Will's old room then?' he asked her.

'We had a long hard think about what we wanted to do with it,' sighed Mum. She was about to say something and the words caught in her throat. She tried to smile at Dougie but her lip quivered, struggling to hold back the emotion. Val reached an arm around her and gave her a comforting hug until she could continue.

'I couldn't keep looking at it, and I should imagine the last thing Will would've wanted was for us to turn it into a shrine, so we cleared it out.'

'That was the *only* thing I wanted! A shrine was just fine – and what've they done with all my posters?' I looked at Dougie, indignantly. He just shook his head.

I wanted to ask Dougie to push Mum for answers. If there was anyone left who might know what was going on, it was Mum. But my mate was well ahead of me.

'You look well, Mrs Underwood. You were so sad the last time I saw you. Understandably, of course.'

Mum gave Dougie a sad, tender smile. 'We were all sad, Douglas. We still are, for that matter. Nothing will ever be the same. Nothing can ever return Will to me.'

'Yet here I am,' I whispered, Dougie shivering at my words as Mum continued.

'I didn't sleep for a week after his death, even with the medicines the doctors prescribed. There were probably enough

114

drugs in me to tranquilise a horse but somehow I kept going. I was in a terrible state, as only a mother could be. Was it my fault that Will was out on his own that night?'

'He wasn't on his—' Dougie began, but Mum cut him off, her eyes wet with tears.

'Look at me. I thought I was done crying. I'll never be done. I loved my boy – I love both of them – but could I have paid more attention? Should I have been stricter, ensured he was in earlier? I mean, it wasn't so late, but I didn't know where he was. What kind of parent does that make me?'

'He was with friends, Mrs Underwood. He was happy. Will was a good lad, he avoided trouble. What happened – it wasn't his fault. And it wasn't yours, either.'

'I know. It was the driver of the car who's responsible.'

Instantly I was transported back to the hit-and-run, my bicycle crumpling under the impact of the car, spinning me into the air. I hadn't thought about it too much, had avoided the memory, the pain. Only then did it occur to me that Mum had been living with the event all this time, reliving it in her own mind, imagining what I'd been through.

'If they ever find the swine who did it, he wants hanging,' added Val.

'That's an argument that we can't get into, Val,' said Mum with a sniff, silencing her neighbour before she could get a rant on. 'An eye for an eye gets us nowhere. But to find out who was behind the wheel and get them behind bars would be some justice. But what chance is there of that ever happening?'

I wanted to hug her, more than I'd ever wanted to in life. You take so much for granted with family. You assume you'll always be there for one another, you don't tell them what they mean to you, always thinking you're going to get the chance to say goodbye, the big death-bed scene. I never got that chance with Mum, and only now did it hit me like a bolt out of the blue.

'I've moved on as best I can, Douglas,' said Mum. 'One has to. To dwell on the past would've served no purpose. I have to celebrate Will's life the only way I know how. I need to live on, for him. Keep him alive in my heart.'

Dougie, bless him, stepped forward to hug her. She was right, he had always been a sensitive soul.

'If only she knew I was here,' I said, as much to myself as Dougie. But there was nothing from her, no awareness, no recognition of my presence. I reached out and ran my hand over her head, my fingers lingering through her hair. My heart ached. She glanced up suddenly. *What was that?*

'Anyway, I just wanted to call by and say hello,' Dougie said, pulling away.

'I'm glad you did,' said Mum. 'You're a good lad, Douglas. Don't be shy about calling round.'

'I won't,' replied Dougie. I knew he probably wouldn't come back. He'd been here for me, not my mother. Had this been the last roll of the dice in our search to find answers? Where did this leave us now? There was only really one place left.

Dougie started for the door, pausing to give my mum one more compliment.

'I like the tracksuit,' he said. 'Are you working out alongside Mr Underwood?'

'Oh no, the box room's all Geoff's. Val and I have been training for a fun run, to raise funds for the children's hospice in town. As I said, I've found a way of celebrating Will's memory and doing some good for other kids in the process.'

'That's awesome,' said Dougie, and he meant it. He even glanced my way and nodded. My heart ballooned now, full of pride for my mum's efforts.

'There's a gang of us, mums from the old school run from when you boys were in short pants. The run's this afternoon at the race course.'

'You could join us,' said Val. 'I'm sure we've got a spare T-shirt in your size.'

'T-shirt?' he asked.

Right on cue, Val and Mum unzipped their tracksuit tops and pulled them open. My school photo from about Year Five was emblazoned on the front of their pristine white T-shirts, crowned with the words *Team Will.* Dougie stifled a laugh.

'Not bad, eh?' said Val. 'Sure you don't want to join us?'

'Very striking, but I'll pass, if that's OK,' Dougie said as he reached back and grabbed the door handle. 'I'm sure if Will were here to see you he'd be very proud.'

'I am here and "proud" isn't a word that springs to mind. It's times like this I'm glad I'm dead.'

The sight of Mum's gang legging it across a racecourse with my face stencilled across them would have likely killed me anyway!

'Make sure you live your life to its fullest, Douglas,' said Mum. 'Don't be afraid of challenges, face up to your worst fears . . . you can do anything, understand me? Regret is a terrible thing.'

Dougie nodded, my mother's words seeming to make him think.

I made for the door, pausing to peck my mum on the cheek. 'Love you, Mum.'

She raised a hand to her face, brushing the skin absentmindedly where I'd kissed her.

'Did you see that?' I said, as Dougie opened the door and I drifted after him. 'I'm sure she felt something there – twice!'

My friend waved as he walked away from the house, setting off down the street. My mum waved back.

'Your mum's a smart lady, mate,' he said, her words still ringing in his ears.

'I need to work on that, the connection thing,' I said excitedly, looking back at Mum on the doorstep as we left my old home behind. 'There's a way of reaching out, of touching things in your world.'

'All good,' said Dougie, with purpose in his stride. 'And in the meantime it's time for me to reach out too. To try and touch someone in your world.'

'What are you saying?'

'The House,' he replied with a fearful shiver. 'I'm ready to return.'

SEVENTEEN

Brighter and Braver

As with many things that induced bowel-wobbling bouts of terror, Red Brook House looked far less scary in daylight. Our last trip had resulted in a twilight flight through the woods, the wailing girl behind us as we screamed and scrambled our way to safety. With the sun now directly overhead and a chill wind at our backs, we stood before the red-brick building eyeing it nervously. The foreboding shadows that had shrouded it the other week were gone now, though they'd be back soon enough when the night came in. The house's façade was crumbling, stained green with decades of moss and lichen where the sun's bright rays couldn't reach. Thick tendrils of twisting ivy snaked across the walls, creeping in through the empty windows and broken brickwork, throttling the life from the structure.

'Can't think why they want to pull this place down . . .' said Dougie.

I didn't answer him, instead approaching the stone steps that led up to the doors. I'd missed it the first time I was here, failed to recognise what could only be described as paranormal activity. There was a tension in the air, an electrical charge that caused my ghostly body to tingle. I'd first noticed the phenomenon in the woodwork class some weeks ago, when I'd struck out at Dougie. It had next happened when we visited my mum – twice on that occasion – a sensation that I was making a connection with the world around me. A similar feeling presently struck me, only it wasn't the living, breathing world I was connecting with: it was the spiritual. It was *my* world.

'You ready for this?' I called back.

'Ready as I'll ever be,' Dougie replied anxiously, wrapped in his trademark parka, plus a hat and scarf in case she tried to freeze him again. 'Let's see if she's got some answers for us.'

He was brave to be returning here. For me, nervous though I was, I didn't feel in physical danger from the phantom girl. I was already dead: could she really harm me? But for Dougie, there was more to be afraid of.

'Stay close,' I said. 'If we find her, I'll do all the talking. If she'll reason with anyone, hopefully it's me.'

'No argument here, buddy,' he said, stepping up to the broken window to the side of the entrance and clambering up on to the sill. He jumped through, landing on the rotten floorboard with a thump, finding me on the other side waiting for him.

The interior of the House was altogether more ruined in the cold light of day. The vines had found their way inside, rooting themselves into every exposed brick, board and beam. Paint peeled away like blistered skin the entire length of the walls, revealing crumbling damp-soaked plaster beneath. The chandelier in the entrance hall jingled suddenly, causing both of us to jump. A pair of birds took off, disappearing with a chorus of shrieks up into the broken ceiling, making for the daylight in a flurry of feathers.

'What do you reckon?' asked Dougie. 'Upstairs? Like the other week?'

'Seems as good a plan as any. She appeared when we started up the staircase, didn't she?'

Side by side, boy and ghost, we set off up the steps. Dougie reached out, gingerly brushing the banister with his hand, feeling for the freezing chill that had burned him on that frightful night. My own eyes were fixed on the landing ahead, awaiting the reappearance of the girl at any moment. My anticipation increased as each step took us higher.

Arriving on to the first floor we looked either way along

the long, dusty corridors. The doors lining each passage were closed, adding to the sense of foreboding hanging over the House. There was no sign of the girl. I turned and looked up, the curving staircase hugging the walls as it rose to the second floor.

'This place is huge,' I said. 'How on earth are we supposed to find her?'

'I was kind of hoping she'd pop up like the Wicked Witch as soon as we hit that first step. This is like pulling teeth. I *hate* waiting for surprises, especially nasty ones!'

'Don't take another step,' I said, pointing to the ground. 'Look. Footprints.'

In the dust on the floor, there was an outline of a large man's shoe. We'd both seen the caretaker here the other week, creeping out of the front door under cover of darkness. What if he was in some way connected to the ghost?

'Borley?' asked Dougie, ahead of me already.

'Unless there's someone else who's been creeping about in here, but I don't see any other disturbances in the dust. Do you?'

We both took a moment, scouring the floor for any telltale marks, but it was quite clear that whoever the footprints belonged to hadn't lingered on the first floor before heading up to the second. We set off in pursuit. A filthy stained-glass window allowed a murky light on to the staircase as we

arrived on the top floor. The rotten floorboards on the landing groaned beneath Dougie's feet. From here the trail in the
dust took us left along a darkened corridor. There, right at the
end, the cold glow of the winter sunlight illuminated a single
open door. I heard Dougie gulp.

'You OK, mate?'

'Just wondering how quickly I can leg it out of here if
things get hairy,' he said, rubbing his throat as if he were
awaiting the hangman's noose.

I reached a reassuring hand out, my insubstantial fingers
hovering in thin air against the shoulder of his green parka
jacket. The two of us laughed nervously.

'Come on,' he said, steeling himself. 'Let's get this over
with.'

We paced down the corridor toward the open door. I kept
glancing at my friend, his fear rolling off him in waves and
adding to my own. By the time the two of us reached the
open doorway we were both terrified of what awaited us.
Peering round the corner of the faded door frame, we looked
into the room.

It had once been a classroom, the large blackboard that
filled the wall still bearing the faded marks of a lesson taught
long ago. A fish tank sat upon a long bench beside the windows at the room's rear, the water within a murky, toxic
sludge by the look of things. No sign of any fish. The desks

remained exactly where they'd been positioned when the House was still a working school, around twenty in neat, orderly lines facing the teacher's desk at the front. Each had a hinged lid, inkwells and ancient messages scrawled across the wooden top. And there, in the centre of a wrought-iron fireplace set into a side wall, was something which pulled us up short.

'Are you seeing that?' asked Dougie.

'The shrine? Yeah. Hard to miss it.'

The pair of us stepped closer to better see it. A collection of candles were positioned in a haphazard circle, their wicks and wax melted down into puddles. Fresh candles had been embedded into the remains of those that had long since died, the occasional coloured one added to the mix to give the pooled remains a marbled look. In the centre of the circle were a collection of books, their edges curling, their jackets battered. Other strange bits and pieces were placed carefully around: a frayed old school tie hung looped from a poker stand, a delicate gold necklace beside it, with a crucifix twinkling in the sunlight. Faded sepia photographs had been carefully arranged at the back of the hearth, while a hockey stick sat on the mantelpiece above.

'Is it me or does this rank as pretty blooming freaky?' asked Dougie as we bent down to look at the collection of oddities.

'It's right up there, mate,' I replied, stepping over toward the window. Beyond, over the bare blackened branches of the treetops, I could see our high school, the modern monstrosity that had condemned the House to the past. I couldn't help but feel sorry for the old building, its walls and hallways rich with stories that would be forever lost when the bulldozers moved in.

Dougie reached down and picked up one of the books, catching one of the candles in the process and dislodging it from the melted wax. He tried to stop it from falling, only succeeding in haplessly knocking more of them loose as they rattled and rolled across the hearth. I winced as I watched him replace them awkwardly.

'Are they in the same place you found them?' I asked.

'Dunno. Does it matter?'

He lifted the book and blew the dust from the jacket. It was an exercise book, its binding creaking as he opened it to examine the contents. I peered over his shoulder to get a closer look, the yellowed pages full of curly script. The occasional blot was the only thing to spoil the neat handwriting, where a nib had leaked its ink. The odd word caught my eye, mention of Cromwell and Charles, monarchs and monasteries.

'A history book,' I said.

'Belonging to . . .' said Dougie, clapping it shut once again so he could read the name on the cover. He squinted, holding it to the light.

'Phyllis Carrington.'

'Yes?' came the sudden voice as we both turned, coming face to face with the girl in the grey pinafore as she appeared in the doorway, blocking our exit.

EIGHTEEN

Intros and Outros

Dougie was scrambling across the floor, back-pedaling into desks and tables as they clattered down upon him. I raised my hands towards the girl in the doorway, half expecting her to unleash another mournful wail, as on our previous meeting. Instead she stepped into the room where we could see her better. Her eyes now sparkled blue, alert and aware. There was nothing monstrous about her: whatever horror had stood on the staircase that awful evening had been replaced by this grey vision of innocence.

'What's the matter with your friend?' she asked me as Dougie stumbled backwards. 'Is he not right in the head?'

'Something like that,' I replied nervously as she stepped further into the room. 'He's always been nervous around . . . ghosts.'

She stopped and looked me up and down. 'He seems all right in *your* company. Perhaps it's girls he's afraid of?'

'You've a point there. His last encounter with the opposite sex left him looking like a shaved panda. Not a good look.'

'For real?' gasped Dougie as he clambered out of the jumble of tumbled furniture. 'You're ganging up on me with her? Need I remind you the last time we met her she almost scared you back to life?'

I studied the girl as she watched my friend straighten himself. He was right, she'd frightened both of us witless the last time we encountered her. The girl before us bore no resemblance to that creature.

'Don't you remember meeting us before?' I asked her.

'Yeah,' added Dougie. 'Why the sudden character shift? Are you schizophrenic or what?'

She stared at us both suspiciously, her brow knitted as she considered us both. Twirling a finger through one of the red ribbons that held her pale blonde hair tied up in bunches, a mischievous smile suddenly spread across her face.

'Oh *that* meeting? Yeah, I remember that, the two of you stumbling up the staircase like Abbott and Costello.'

'Abbott and what?' asked Dougie.

'Comedians from old black-and-white movies,' I explained. 'My dad has a collection of them on DVD.'

'Deevee what?' countered the girl.

'OK, hang on,' I said. 'I think we need to clear a couple of things up. Firstly, why did you wail at us when we first met one another? We didn't come here looking for trouble, we came searching for answers. Local superstitions said the House was haunted and for once they were right. So why the horror show?'

'You're new to ghosthood, aren't you?' she said. I nodded as she continued. 'The scares comes with the territory, for me, anyway. I like my own company. I don't need people snooping around here. For anyone to return even after I've given them the old "black eyes" routine tells me they're serious about wanting to meet me. I wouldn't have harmed you, if that's what you're concerned about.'

'You froze me half to death!' Dougie was glaring at her in disbelief, but I found myself smiling. I was warming to her, and quickly too.

'So that was all for show?' asked Dougie.

'Seemed to do the trick,' she sighed, perching herself on the edge of one of the desks. 'Must be some big questions you need answering to have come back after that.'

'But you knew I was a ghost, right?' I said. 'Yet you were still happy to put the frights on me and see me disappear with my mate?'

'You're green,' she said. 'It's written all over you, I saw it straight away. You're still thinking like a lifer. You haven't been cold long enough to get your head round it all, but it's not my job to walk you through it. I had to muddle my own way along. You can learn the ropes yourself.'

'The ropes?'

'How to control your powers.'

'I don't need you to show me how to control anything. I just want to find out why I haven't moved on and left this limbo behind me.'

'And you think I can help you?' she giggled. 'Don't you think *I'd* have moved on if I knew what it was that was stopping me? We're all trapped here for whatever reasons, with our own curses keeping us tethered to the living world. No one ghost is in the same boat as the next, friend.'

I considered her words as Dougie stepped across to the window and peered outside.

'So it's Phyllis, right?' I asked. 'Do you really have no idea why you're here? Not even a suspicion? It seems like you've been here a while. How did you . . . die?'

Phyllis opened her mouth as if she were about to answer, and then paused. Her face was deathly pale already, but if it was possible to drain of colour any more, it did so right then. Her playful expression was gone in an instant, replaced by one of fear and anxiety.

'What's the matter?' I said, reaching out to brush her arm with my fingertips. There was an actual physical sensation as

131

we touched, Phyllis looking up as I gave her a squeeze of encouragement. Dougie interrupted before I could say anything more.

'He's back,' gasped my mate from where he stood at the window. 'We need to go, and now!'

Dougie was off and running, not waiting to say goodbye to Phyllis, and I was torn away from her as he sped off down the corridor, only able to shout one last thing back at her as we ran.

'We'll be back, I promise!'

Dougie was bounding down the stairs two and three at a time now, hugging the banister as he hit the first and then ground floor.

'Where is he?' I gasped as he stumbled across the lobby of the House, past the double doors. Dougie pointed frantically at the entrance, his eyes wide with terror at the sound of a key sliding into the lock. The mechanism rattled before a sudden *clunk* told us the door was unlocked. Dougie was already in the side room, waiting to leap out of the window and be on his way. Timing was everything: Borley had to be entering into the House at the very moment Dougie was exiting. If Dougie got it wrong, he was bound to be caught.

As the double doors opened, groaning on their hinges, Dougie was on his way. Down he went, dragging his legs over the splintered windowsill, face first towards the ground where he landed with a crunch, half the frame coming away with him. He scrambled to his feet, shaking loose the shards of rotten wood before heading for the drive. His run was stumbling, a limp dogging his escape as he clutched his right thigh.

'You there!'

He was hot on our heels, the old man skipping down the steps on spry feet before giving chase.

'He's catching you up,' I warned Dougie, alerting him to the caretaker's pursuit. 'The woods!'

Immediately he peeled away from the gravel drive and ducked between trunk and branch, heading deeper into the undergrowth.

'C'mere, boy!' shouted Borley, following us into the woods.

Limping, Dougie slipped between the trees, picking his way towards the railings that encircled the grounds. I looked back all the while, keeping my eye on my friend's hunter, unhindered by the trees and bushes that blocked the path. I could see Borley's face twisting with anger as he tried to catch up, cursing as the branches and brambles lashed his flesh.

'How's your leg?' I asked.

'A mere scratch,' Dougie whispered, removing a six-inch dagger of wood that had punctured through the fabric of his jeans. I knew instantly that with a slashed leg he'd have little chance of making it over the railings.

'Follow the fence round to the gate; try and lose Borley in the undergrowth.'

'Easier said than done,' he panted, resting his back against a tree. 'Where is he?'

I looked past him, spying the old man maybe twenty feet away, drawing ever closer. I could sense Dougie's anxiety coming off him in waves, and I shared his fear. I couldn't allow Borley to find him; I had to do what I could to help him escape. An idea was slowly forming.

'Stay where you are,' I said, drifting away from him directly toward Borley. 'Run when I shout.'

I was past the caretaker in an instant, moving as far away as possible from Dougie. Although our special bond gave me strength, it also proved a hindrance. I'd been happy to become Dougie's shadow, close by at all times, but it seemed I now depended upon him. My friend had become the centre of my world and the further I strayed from him, the weaker I became. Just as I felt the elastic connection between us stretched to its absolute limit, I braced myself, letting my anger build. I stared at Borley, my eyes drilling into the back of his head as he scoured the woods for my mate. The connection between the caretaker and Phyllis was all too obvious to me. He *had* to know about Phyllis: why else was he here, at the House? Was it his shrine? And what part had he played in her death? The misery at my own fate was now surging to the fore, my anger at the driver of the car who stole my life away clouding my emotions. I let it build to a crescendo, the snapping of a twig bringing my focus back to Borley.

My hand lashed out, striking the branches beside me and sending them rattling against one another. The strange ectoplasm flew from the twisted twigs like threads of a spider's web, coating the gnarled branches where I'd struck them. Instantly the caretaker's head spun about.

'That you, lad?' he called out, weather-beaten face wrinkling as he narrowed his eyes. He set off in my direction, picking his way over to where the noise had sounded.

'Go now!' I shouted, confident that Borley had taken the bait.

As Dougie set off, I followed after him. I drifted past the caretaker as he continued toward where I'd been, snarling at the old geezer as I passed him by. Dougie hurried on, not daring to look back, as he flitted and fell between tree and bush on his way to the exit. The distraction had bought him just enough time to get out of the woods, and a few more precious seconds to navigate through the chained gates. He hit the grille and pushed hard, the metal links once again straining as he forced them apart.

'C'mere!' shouted Borley, as he burst out of the undergrowth at our backs, hurrying towards us. He reached out, his fingertips brushing the fur of my mate's hood as Dougie collapsed between the gates and through to the other side. He bounced off the bonnet of the caretaker's van, which was parked at the head of the drive, leaving a bloody handprint on its side. Borley rattled the gates before searching his pockets for the keys, cursing out loud. He'd have no luck finding them: I'd seen him leave them in the door to the House.

'Now would be a good time to get going, Dougie,' I said.

'I saw you, boy!' Borley shouted as my friend hobbled down the road, putting distance between us and the horrible old man. 'I saw you!'

NINETEEN

Questions and Answers

'You done something to your leg, Hancock?'

Dougie winced as he sat down in the chair before the head-master's desk. We'd spent the previous Sunday afternoon cleaning up his injury. I say we, but it was basically me wittering in his ear while Dougie washed, cleaned and dressed the wound. A thick layer of bandage – enough to clothe an Egyptian mummy – encircled his right thigh, his trousers now stretched to ripping point.

'It's nothing, sir. I took a bang to it falling out of a tree in my garden.'

'Are you sure it's not a sport injury from, say . . . hockey?' asked Mr Goodman, raising an eyebrow as my friend settled.

'Phew,' I said, voicing Dougie's relief. 'He's heard about your chat with Lucy.'

Initially, we'd assumed he'd been called into Goodman's office to explain what he'd been doing at the House. We'd spent the night talking it over, going through the various events that might occur. Most worrying had been if Borley had gone straight to Goodman, reporting my mate for breaking and entering. An angry Goodman was a thing to behold: legend had it he once picked a boy up by his sideburns and threw him into a bin for answering back. Borley keeping our sneaking secret had been the best possible outcome, at least until the old man eventually challenged Dougie over his shenanigans. That would no doubt be out of earshot of Goodman, and would bring its own problems. As it transpired, invading Miss Roberts' hockey session had been the reason for the summons.

'That's right, lad,' said the headmaster, turning his back to Dougie as he looked out of the window. 'I heard all about your nonsense on the hockey field. There are few things in life that I'm scared of. Being buried alive is one. *Jaws* has stopped me from swimming in the sea since a Christmas cinema trip in 1975. And an irate Miss Roberts: the thought of that one tops the lot. You mind telling me what business you had interrupting her hockey trials?'

Dougie cleared his throat, stalling for time. He glanced to

where I stood by the door. I shrugged. This line of questioning hadn't been something we'd considered.

'I had to speak with Lucy Carpenter, sir,' he said. 'It was important.'

'So important it couldn't wait until you got out of school?' shouted Goodman, spinning round and hitting the desk with his fists. 'I hear you were hanging around the girls' classes last week like a dog sniffing out a bone. Am I running some sort of dating service here now or what? Last time I looked it was a high school I was charged with managing, unless you know better, Hancock? Well? You so keen on the poor lass that you'd risk irritating me?'

Everything about Goodman's voice told me that Dougie was in serious trouble here. The string of quick-fire questions was the headmaster's favourite style of attack, the challenges issued in such rapid succession that the victim had no chance of answering them.

'Spit it out, boy! Cat got your tongue? Getting shy all of a sudden? Girl talk not something you're used to, Hancock? Preferring spying on them from the bushes than talking to them in person? Is that it?'

'It's ... it's not like that, sir!' Dougie said at last, finally getting a word in edgeways. 'I wasn't stalking her! Whatever Miss Roberts said, it's not true—'

'Miss Roberts a liar now, is she, Hancock? That's quite an accusation, lad!'

'No, sir, that's not what I'm saying at all. She's just got the wrong end of the stick!'

'You're lucky she didn't give *you* the wrong end of the hockey stick. If she catches hold of you, she may yet still!'

'I don't get the chance to speak to Lucy during school-time, certainly not alone, as we aren't in the same classes for everything, and when I *do* see her she's always got her mates around her.'

'So during a hockey match was obviously the next best opportunity to chat her up?'

Dougie shrugged hopelessly. Goodman had a point. I'd warned Dougie at the time that his plan was as about as foolproof as his goth impression, but he hadn't listened. It wasn't even like Dougie intended to return to Lucy anyway – she'd made her feelings about me known quite clearly. The headmaster continued.

'Can't talk to her outside of school either, Hancock? Are you some kind of mumbling halfwit who's scared of anything that giggles?'

I snorted at that, and Dougie briefly glared my way before returning his gaze to the headmaster.

'Don't worry, sir. I'm done talking to girls. It won't happen again.'

'Good lord, Hancock,' gasped Goodman, raising his hands to his cheeks and pulling a pantomime face of fear. 'Not *scared* of girls, are you, lad?'

'No, sir,' Dougie replied, his face crimson with embarrassment. 'It's not like that. Vinnie Savage is always hanging around her anyway. He used to date her.'

Goodman's face slipped now, his mocking tone fading as he frowned. 'Right. Well. Savage is a toe-rag, I can see how that might provide problems.' He sat down and leaned back in his leather captain's chair, staring hard at Dougie who cowered across the desk from him.

'I'll give you a tip, lad,' said Goodman at last. 'A pointer from my own arsenal of how to deal with people. Next time you see a lass and like the look of her, stop cowering and sneaking about like some timid wee muppet and go straight up to her. Faint hearts never won fair lady and all that.'

'But what about the Savages of this world?'

'That lad's a bully, Hancock. If he gives you grief, you tell me and I'll see how he likes it when the boot's on the other foot.'

'And what if he hits me?'

'You hit him back, Hancock. Good grief, I can't do everything for you. You need to stand up for yourself, lad. Stop being such a pushover. Stop letting other people walk over you.'

Dougie shifted nervously.

'Am I still in trouble with Miss Roberts?'

'I'll see if I can tame that particular beast,' Goodman

replied, shuffling the papers on his desk. 'A bit of well-placed flattery and the promise of an early finish might douse that fire. You don't get to where I am without knowing how to treat the ladies. Don't let me see you back here, Hancock.'

He looked up, eyes bulging.

'Well, lad? Why are you still here?'

'That's your cue to go, mate,' I said, hovering by the door and waiting for Dougie to join me. He wasted no more time, hopping to his feet. Instantly he winced, the pain of his bandaged thigh catching him unawares again.

'Nasty business, that cramp,' said Goodman quietly as Dougie limped gingerly to the door. 'Maybe get Mrs Jolly to take a look at it, eh? Give your thigh a massage. That'll get you moving again.'

I chuckled at the thought of that, my laughter for Dougie's ears alone as he turned the door handle.

'One last thing, Hancock,' came Goodman's voice from behind. Dougie turned, hovering in the doorway. The headmaster was looking down as his big red pen marked the papers on his desk, his bald pate reflecting the glow of the ceiling light.

'Yes, sir?'

'What business do you have at the House?'

'Beg your pardon, sir?'

Dougie and I looked at one another in horror. He *knew* my

142

friend had been there, and he'd waited until now to say something. Had Borley grassed Dougie up? Goodman continued without looking up.

'I think you heard me well enough. What's your fascination with the House?'

'Don't mention Borley,' I hissed. 'Not yet! Not until you've got more evidence!'

Dougie cleared his throat as Goodman's red pen squeaked across the paperwork.

'I think ... the place is haunted.'

'Nice one,' I said, slow handclapping beside him. 'That won't send alarm bells ringing.'

Goodman snorted. 'Haunted houses? I've heard the stories, but I thought you'd have more sense than to hold with that rot, Hancock. You believe what you want, but how gullible do you think I am?'

'I saw the ghost of a girl, sir,' said Dougie, irked by the headmaster's dismissive tone. 'Her name's Phyllis.'

'Shut up blabbing, you cretin,' I gasped as Goodman stopped scribbling. He looked up slowly, eyes fixed on my pal.

'It sounds to me, Hancock, that you're still not right after that bad business with Will Underwood.'

I jumped at the mention of my name. Goodman was still glaring coldly at my friend.

'I get that you miss your friend, but this has to stop. Chasing non-existent ghosts, looking for answers where you'll only put yourself in danger? Do I need to get you referred to a child psychologist, Hancock? I've a letter lying in my desk drawer just waiting for my signature. Must I have you removed from the school until you're well enough to return? If ever?'

'No, sir,' Dougie replied with a nervous shudder.

'Don't you dare let me find you've been back to the House. That place has been condemned, for good reason too: it's dangerous, understand?'

'Yes, sir.'

'Grand,' replied Goodman. 'Now get going, Hancock. And remember: I'll be watching you.'

TWENTY

Scratching and Scuttling

'You're risking a lot, being back here tonight after what Goodman said today.'

Dougie turned on the stairs, shining his torch towards me out of habit. Dazzling though the light was, the beam cut straight through me, illuminating the tattered walls of the entrance hall.

'You'd rather I turned back?'

'God, no. I appreciate you returning, especially if Goodman is keeping an eye on you. Do you think he really does have a letter there that can get you sectioned? You have to admit your actions must look pretty odd to others, ever since I died. People are talking and Goodman is listening.'

Dougie shivered, his breath clouding before the snorkel of his parka.

'It's not Goodman I'm worried about. Keep your eyes peeled for Borley.'

'Phyllis!' I called up the flight of steps, waiting for her to appear on the landing, but she didn't show.

'I don't like this,' said Dougie.

'Let's keep moving. Head to the classroom. Perhaps we'll find her there.'

We passed the first floor, moving on up to the second. The House transformed once again from the daylight ruin to a twilight nightmare. Intermittently we'd call out her name, pausing to see if she'd answer back or materialise, but there was no sign of her. The torch's light penetrated the gloom, the glow keeping the darkness at bay momentarily before it swallowed us once more. Indistinct scuttling and scratching sounds emanated from all around; beneath the floorboards, from in the attic, behind the rotting panels that clung to the walls.

'I hate rats. I've told you that before, right? I kid you not, Will, if you ever fancy becoming a hardcore ghost, you could move into this place tomorrow,' said Dougie, his unblinking eyes focusing on the path ahead. 'It's a ready-made haunted house, complete with resident rodents!'

'Can't see that ever happening,' I replied as we arrived on the top floor. 'I'm still jumping at my own shadow. Don't think I've got what it takes to genuinely scare anyone.'

'Boo!'

Dougie hit the deck, with me alongside him, the pair of us taken by surprise as Phyllis appeared suddenly through the wall of the corridor, her ethereal shimmer lighting the room. While my friend clutched his chest, his torch rolling across the floorboards, I drifted back to my feet and confronted her.

'You know, for someone who's been starved of human contact, you're not making much effort to ingratiate yourself. We nearly ended up with *three* ghosts there.'

'Oh don't be such a silly,' replied Phyllis. 'I was only playing. What's the point of being a ghost if you can't dish out a scare every now and again?'

'Putting the frights on folk?'

'It's there in the job description,' she said. 'Seems you never received your handbook.'

'There's a handbook?'

'Good grief. Of course there isn't!'

She floated off down the corridor, her pale smoky feet brushing the ground as she went.

'Hang on a minute,' I said, rushing after her. I grabbed her by the arm, the connection solid, at least between the two of us. She turned, wide-eyed, as I pulled her back towards me. 'You need to be nicer to people.'

'Who are you to tell me what I should or shouldn't do?' she

replied, tugging herself free. 'You're lucky, you have your friend there. I've got nobody.'

'You've got us,' I said.

We stared at one another as Dougie stomped down the corridor after us.

'I'm sorry,' she said, her voice a whisper. 'I didn't mean to upset anyone. You're the first people I've been able to speak to since ... well, for ever. I guess I might be a little stir-crazy, locked up in here for who knows how many years.'

'Let me get this straight, then,' said Dougie as we entered the classroom. 'Will seems to be connected to me, for whatever reason—'

'Love,' I cut in with a grin as he waved me to be silent.

'But it's the House that you're tied to. You haunt this place, right?'

'Well, I've never tried to leave,' she said, thinking on that for a moment. 'Never saw the need to or felt the desire. I'm bound to the House.'

'Another one for your *Rules of Ghosting* handbook, chum,' I said with a smile. I turned to Phyllis. 'I'm not joking, by the way. He's been taking notes.' I was keeping things light, but it was clear that Dougie was into this now. My friend continued.

'And do all ghosts have the same connections to people and places?'

'Don't know,' she answered. 'You'd have to ask them.'

'Do you know . . . others?' asked Dougie, excitedly.

'I know they're out there, just as I detected Will.' She paused and looked out of the window. 'You know the old train station, beyond the woods?' She pointed in the direction she meant. 'I remember hearing that was haunted when *I* was a child. A Victorian lamplighter, they said. Went crazy and started snuffing out lives instead of lanterns. Threw himself under a train when the police tried to catch him.'

Dougie and I both shivered.

'I know he's there,' she whispered. 'I can . . . sense him.'

'That's one thing I meant to ask, Phyllis,' said Dougie. 'How is it you can talk to me? Do I have a connection with you like I've got with Will or what?'

'It's not about me, Dougie,' said Phyllis. 'It's about you. You've got something special with Will, you can see and hear him with zero effort. I reckon that's left you tuned in.'

'Tuned in?'

'I think I've got this,' I replied, turning to my mate as the three of us walked into Phyllis' classroom. 'Since you got used to talking to me, it's left you open to everything else out there that might be ghostly. You're on the same wavelength now. You can pick up on things regular people can't. I bet you can hear dog-whistles too!'

Dougie glowered at me as Phyllis continued.

'You can sense activity from the other side, the spirit world. Your perception has shifted. I've no idea how long it'll last, but for now you're getting the best of both worlds.'

'If this is the best, I'd hate to see the worst,' muttered Dougie grumpily, scuffing the floor with his foot.

'So how do you manage to scare regular people?' I said, ignoring him. 'If they can't actually see you, how does that work?'

Phyllis sat herself down at a desk. I joined her, while Dougie walked over to the window.

'If I concentrate, I can affect things in his world,' she said, pointing at Dougie. 'If I focus on a desired effect, I can some-times make it happen. Temperature shifts, rising wind, eerie noises and that – they're what I can control. It usually hap-pens when I feel threatened. Emotion seems to be the trigger.'

'Can I do this too?' I asked.

'I don't know; have you tried?'

'Well, I've sort of made things move when I was really angry, but not very well.'

'Your dad punches kittens,' Dougie called over, 'and your nan's got a moustache like a walrus!'

'What the—?'

'I'm trying to help, give you that little push to get you mad.'

'Sounds like you've kissed my nan,' I replied, suspiciously.

'Seriously, mate, I think it needs to be more natural than that. Right, Phyllis?'

The girl nodded, her red ribbons bobbing as her blonde pigtails fluttered. I thought back to striking out, hitting things when Dougie or I felt emotional: back in the wood-work room, the can of pop with Bloody Mary, Dougie's bedside lamp, the branches when we were being chased by Borley.

'Come to think of it, when I *have* been upset, certain things have happened.'

'Like what?' Phyllis asked, keen to hear more. 'Cold? Wind? What?'

'I was able to connect with things, physically.'

'You can manipulate solid objects in the real world, by touch?'

'Can't you do that?'

'No,' she said excitedly. 'And I thought I knew all there was to know about this ghostly lark! Perhaps it's you who should be teaching me!'

'I'll warn you now,' said Dougie, 'he comes with added ectoplasm. It ain't pretty.'

I thought back to the business in the woods, the fear I'd felt for Dougie. I worried about what Borley might do if he caught my friend. Maybe Phyllis knew something more about the old caretaker?

'You say you've been stuck here, in the House, for years,' I said. 'How many exactly?'

'It all blurs really. I kept count at first but soon the days merged into weeks, then became months and years. I stopped counting after a while.' Her voice was quiet now, wistful as she thought back to a time well past.

'What year were you born in?' I asked her.

'Nineteen fifty-one,' she replied.

Both Dougie and I gasped, suddenly realising her age.

'You'd be in your sixties if you were still alive today,' said my friend.

'Sharp, Dougie,' I said. 'You always were a wizard at counting. Did you work that out without taking your socks off?'

Dougie looked at Phyllis as an antique dealer might appraise an auction item. 'You must be, what, twelve years old?'

'I was thirteen when I died,' said Phyllis indignantly, clearly proud of the fact she'd reached her teenage years. 'I remember that much. The Beatles were number one in the charts again, the third time that year: *I Feel Fine*. It was snowing . . .'

Dougie and I looked at one another. We were getting somewhere. She was starting to piece the jigsaw together, thinking about stuff that had been long forgotten. Her death and Borley were connected somehow, I was sure of it. I moved in front of her, catching her attention.

'Three number one hits that year?' I said, trying to guess the rest. 'Reckon that puts us at the back end of the year. So that was probably around December time if it was snowing. It's winter now, Phyllis, which means we're approaching the anniversary.'

'Anniversary?' she whispered.

'Of your death,' replied Dougie quietly.

She was silent, her eyes staring off into space as we waited for her to speak. Dougie's teeth chattered as he raised his hands to his lips, cupping them and blowing into them. I watched as the glass wall of the murky fish tank seemed to crystallise, a spider's web of frost spreading across the surface.

'Perhaps it's already been and gone?' I said, holding her hands in my own as I searched her face for answers.

'No,' she said, her brow knitted as she tried to think. 'It was before Christmas. It was at the end of the year.'

She looked around the classroom, as if someone had entered.

'What is it?' I asked, following her gaze as it flitted between the tables and back toward the teacher's desk. 'What's the matter?'

'It was here . . .' she whispered.

'What do you know about Mr Borley?' said Dougie, unable to stifle the question any longer.

She snapped back to us suddenly, her pale face trembling.

'Borley?'

'What's his secret, Phyllis?' Dougie asked. 'What did he do to you?'

The ghostly girl vanished in the blink of an eye. The room suddenly plunged into darkness. Dougie had flicked the switch on his torch and was now hugging the window frame's edge while he looked outside.

'What is it?' I asked him.

'The woods,' he replied. 'I'm sure I saw a light. Another torch perhaps? There's someone out there, mate. Come on, we'd better get going.'

I followed my friend as he dashed from the empty class-room, leaving a host of unanswered questions hanging in our wake.

TWENTY-ONE

Wheels and Waltzers

'Danger Night! Danger Night! All rides a pound!'

The steady stream of kids crowded through the open gates before spilling giddily into the fairground. For fifty-one weeks of the year this was just a scrap of wasteland beside the railway station, the domain of dog walkers and amorous couples. For that other week of the year it was transformed into a noisy, colourful world of spinning cups, posturing boys and shrieking girls. When the fair came to town you were guaranteed excitement, especially on the opening night. It was named Danger Night on account of the rumour that none of the rides had been safety tested. The cheap prices were a reflection on this. You took your life in your own hands on Danger Night, apparently.

Dougie was stood outside the arcade, the flashing lights of

shoot-em-ups and racing games dancing across his back. Our roleplaying compadre Andy Vaughn stood beside him, blowing into his cupped hands. It was a bitterly cold night, the weather having really turned since we'd fled the House earlier. If there *had* been anyone in the woods outside – and I wasn't convinced there was – then they'd clearly missed Dougie as he'd slipped out of the old building, skipping down the gravel drive on one leg before making good his getaway. We'd got somewhere with Phyllis, of that there was no doubt. She'd explained a bit about being a ghost, and we'd pricked some distant memory which explained how she'd come to haunt the House. The resultant revelations that had risen from the brief conversation had only spawned more questions. Did Phyllis know how she died? Did she know Borley? How were the two connected?

'Scooby Doo never had it this difficult,' said Dougie, leaning against the tent wall of the arcade tent, a supporting post flat to his back. He had his little black notebook out, scribbling away with his pencil.

'Mystery solving? Aye, you're not wrong,' I replied. 'It probably helped that there were no real ghosts in Scooby's world. It was always some mad fairground worker . . .'

'Or a crazy janitor,' added Dougie miserably, the dig not missed by me.

'You're talking to yourself again,' said Andy, clapping his

hands and rubbing them together. Dougie had bumped into Andy and Stu upon arrival at the fair, our friends having already blown most of the money they'd brought in the arcade.

'No, I'm not,' said Dougie, winking at him.

'Ah,' replied Andy. 'You're talking to Will, then? He's here, right?'

'I've told you, he's always here.'

'Whatcha got there, then?' asked Andy, peering over the top of the black book to see what Dougie was writing.

'It's my *Rules on Ghosting*. I find it's the best way of getting my head round how this ghostly business works.'

'And what have you put in there so far?'

The nerd in Dougie needed no more coaxing.

'I've listed the different stages of "ghosthood" Will has gone through, from the earliest moment he realised he was dead. I've recorded every instance where he's made a physical connection with something in the living world. I'm also trying to make sense of the limitations that exist for him. At the moment I'm categorising the different kinds of hauntings that are out there.'

'This sounds more like a Dungeon Master's rulebook,' said Andy, excitedly, his own inner geek leaping proudly to the fore. 'If you need a hand editing it, give me a shout. Can I take a look sometime?'

'Sure,' grinned Dougie.

'Nice to see you smile, mate,' I said to him before turning to Andy. 'Also good to see we have the sceptic on board. He's finally warming to the idea I'm now a ghost as opposed to a figment of your overactive imagination.'

Dougie smiled once more. 'Is he finished in there yet?'

I drifted through the wall of the tent and took a peek, searching for our other friend. Stu was stood beside the coin cascade, a waterfall of ten-pence pieces threatening to spill over and hit the win tray at any moment. The husky chap who worked the change till had an eye on him: the cascade had a way of attracting opportunist thieves, and Stu clearly had that look about him. The torn-gut intestine spill T-shirt he wore hardly meant you could miss him. I watched as he kissed his final coin and posted it into the slot, the coin coming to a halt on the top shelf before sending a further three down on to the next one. As the shelf slid back, the coins pushed against the amassed ledge of silver. I could sense Stu's tension as he waited for the jackpot that never came. I didn't hang around to witness his temper tantrum, although his barrage of cursing could be heard from beyond the canvas walls of the arcade.

'Is that him spent up then or what?' asked Dougie, rubbing his thigh. Before I could answer we heard the ringing of alarm bells from within the tent. A moment later Stu appeared around the side of the makeshift building, shoving handfuls of coins into his pockets.

'For the son of an Oxbridge grad vicar, you can be an awful idiot, Stu,' sighed Dougie.

'Howay, Dougie, quit your gum-bumping and gimme your jacket,' he said. 'That fat lad with the moobs in the change booth saw what I was up to. He's on his way. Need a disguise, dude!'

Reluctantly, Dougie removed his parka and tossed it to Stu, who proceeded to slope off into the throng.

'Cheers, big ears!' he hollered.

'I want it back,' Dougie replied over the sea of heads. 'I'm freezing my arse off here!'

This exclamation drew a crowd of heads turning our way, just as the change vendor came waddling out of the arcade, closing the tent flaps behind him. He looked one way and then the other, jowly face fixed in a fierce frown before loping off into the mob in search of Stu.

'I'm going to follow Stu,' said Andy. 'See if I can prevent him getting into any *more* trouble, ce soir.'

He made a gangster handshake with Dougie then bumped fists, the ungroovy duo's parting gesture drawing a smile from me. If there was ever a pair of souls who shouldn't engage in street slang and stylings, it was this pair. Then Andy did something very sweet. He clicked his fingers and pointed at thin air. It wasn't where I was stood but at least it was an approximation.

'Later, *dudes*,' he said with a wink. He might not have been looking at me, but it was the thought that counted.

'So,' I said, as we watched our Dungeon Master disappear into the crowd, 'what do we do about Borley?'

'What *can* we do about him?' Dougie asked, pocketing his notebook and setting off on a meander through the fairground. The Big Wheel turned as we passed by, screeching girls adding to the cacophony of Danger Night as they went round in their swinging seats. Stopping by a sweet stall, Dougie picked up a toffee apple while I tried to figure out a plan of action.

'You could report what we think we know to Goodman, although I'm not sure whether he'll be in listening mood. He wasn't a happy bunny when you left him and was quite clear about you staying away from the House. Anyway, what do we really think we know? That Borley was involved in the death of Phyllis Carrington somehow? That's a bit of a leap, isn't it?'

'It's a pretty safe leap if you ask me,' said Dougie as he walked away from the stall, taking a bite from his apple. 'Borley's got something to do with Phyllis. How do you think that creepy little shrine got there? We already know she can't move things in my world, so she certainly didn't set it up. It's his handiwork, that's my guess.'

'OK, so maybe seeing Goodman wouldn't be the best course of action, not until we can get more evidence anyway.'

'Evidence? Steady on, Miss Marple. Why the sudden need to turn detective?'

'Well it's not like I'm having much luck discovering why *I'm* still here – perhaps unravelling the mystery of Phyllis' death is the first step toward solving my own?'

Dougie shrugged and nodded, accepting my reasoning.

'How can we do that? Where would we go for evidence?'

I thought for a moment as we came to a halt beside the Waltzers barrier, the cars whizzing by, their occupants threatening to throw up over us at any moment. Neither of us knew where Borley lived. What did that leave us with?

'His office,' I said. 'The caretaker's office at school. That's where we need to look.'

'But he's in there all day, and when he isn't there it's locked up.'

'Then we go at night,' I said. 'It wouldn't be the first time we had a scamper across the school rooftops, would it?'

Dares had been a rites of passage for all my friends over the years, climbing on to the roof of lower school in broad daylight in view of the staff room. We both knew there was a skylight over Borley's office. I say office, it was little more than a broom cupboard. But it was *his* domain. He near enough lived in that small room.

'I feel sick, and it's not the toffee apple,' said Dougie.

'Could be watching the Waltzers,' I said as the ride came to a halt and the riders disembarked.

'I know what it is,' said Dougie, tossing the slightly chewed apple into the mud. 'It's the thought of climbing into Borley's office. I'm afraid of what we'll find there, not least if he comes back.'

'That's why we go at night,' I said. 'The school's like a graveyard after dark.'

'Yet more death-related chit-chat,' he mumbled. 'You're not helping my confidence, Will.'

'Talking to yourself, Hancock?'

We both turned, realising all too late that Vinnie Savage and two of his moronic mates had crept up on Dougie. He trembled as they gathered around him.

'You scared, Hancock?' asked Savage, his big stupid grin crumpling the bum-fluff tash that sat on his lip.

'Regretting lending my jacket to someone, is all,' replied Dougie, giving his arms a rub as they stared him down. 'If you're going to do something, just get it over with, will you?'

'Do something?' said Savage, looking to his cohorts as they guffawed. 'Do you like getting a smack, or what? I heard you were a sicko but I didn't know just how sick.'

'Sicko?' replied Dougie.

'Yeah,' sneered Savage. 'Hanging around in the bushes,

spying on the girls playing hockey? I should beat you up for stalking my Lucy.'

Dougie suddenly raised his hands.

'If you're gonna beat me up, then do it for being a nerd by all means, but not for staring at girls. It's not what you think! I just wanted to talk to her!'

'And the rest,' snarled Savage, stepping closer through the mud. The colourful lights of the fairground suddenly blinked out as the gang leader towered over my mate, plunging him into shadow. He lashed out and Dougie went down into the mud, clutching his shoulder.

'I didn't know she was your Lucy!' he moaned. 'I thought you weren't together any more!'

'We will be again, before long.'

I'd heard enough. I couldn't stand there and watch this bully, this idiot who had made my own school years a misery whenever our paths crossed, torment my best friend any longer. Years of pent-up frustration boiled over, my fury at Savage for his reign of cruelty exploding in the form of a single punch. I caught Savage square in the stomach, up from below where he stood over Dougie. His feet left the floor as he was propelled backward, landing with a mighty splash in a puddle. His mates stood to one side, looking down at him as he struggled in vain to rise before falling back into the dirty water.

Dougie didn't hang around to see what came next. He was off and running – not for the first time that night – finding the crowd once again. Within moments we were in the heart of the sea of teenagers, carried away on a tide of candyfloss, working our way to the exit.

Racing ever closer to the train station.

TWENTY-TWO

Light and Shadow

The noises of Danger Night drifted through the darkness, carried on to the platform by a chill wind. The sounds of music and merrymaking pervaded the air, muffled and muted by the old railway station building that loomed over the tracks like a monster. This old track linked Liverpool to Manchester, and as such saw plenty of traffic during the daytime. At night, it was a different world, the occasional stopper calling in to deposit weary commuters after dark. For tonight, the last train had been and gone. The main gates were locked. The platform was deserted, the station abandoned until morning.

Dougie remained flat to the wall, badly hidden in the alcove beside the entrance to the ticket office. His eyes shone, wide and fearful, as he peeked down the platform to where he'd hurdled the fence. Voices could be heard, far closer than the fairground, his pursuers still clearly searching for him. If they decided to investigate the station, they'd be sure to find him. Dougie was panting, his breath steaming like he'd swallowed a miniature steam engine.

'Got it,' I said, gesturing to the *chuff chuff* clouds that escaped his blue lips. 'Thomas the Tank Engine. Next impression, please!'

'You're hilarious,' he whispered. 'I'm really regretting giving my parka to Stu right now. Make yourself useful. Take a step back and tell me can you see them?'

I backed away from him, safe in the knowledge that nobody could see me. I was able to move perhaps twenty feet or so away from him, comfortably, before feeling the need to come to a halt. I looked down the line to where the fence separated the car park from the platform. I could see shadows approaching, figures illuminated by the fairground at their backs. I recognised Vinnie Savage's voice instantly, his angry snarls peppered by a string of profanities. A hand grabbed the fence and gave it a shake. I held my breath, waiting for one of his bloodhounds to jump the barrier and land on the platform, but he never came. Another voice called him away, leading the search elsewhere, off poor old Dougie's scent.

'We're clear,' I said, and instantly my friend collapsed

against the wall, sliding down the brickwork until his bottom hit the floor. He placed his hand over his chest.

'I don't know about Thomas the Tank Engine,' he shivered. 'My heart's hammering away like a runaway train! You showed some fight back there. Where did that come from?'

'Goodman's little talk,' I said as his breathing began to level out. 'Decided it was time to strike back.'

'Didn't know you had it in you.'

'Neither did I, mate,' I said, as he struggled to rise. 'It's what friends do: you'd have done the same had the roles been reversed. Let's just hope Vinnie thinks the punch came from you, eh?'

I glanced back down the platform, suddenly spying that we weren't as alone as we thought we'd been.

'Hang on a mo,' I said, raising my hand and warding him away. 'Back up. There's somebody on the platform.'

'Where?' he hissed.

I peered down the station house's length as Dougie once more assumed his position in the shadows, hugging the crumbling wall.

'Who is it?' he asked frantically, his voice thin and desperate. 'Is it Savage?'

'Hush!' I said, stepping out of the darkness again, invisible to the living world.

The stranger sat on one of the benches that faced the rails.

Judging by the length of his legs which were extended across the paved ground, the stranger was a man, but more than that was difficult to ascertain. The whole station was shrouded in gloom, the building casting long shadows right across the tracks. It was impossible to see any more from where I stood.

'Don't say a word,' I said to Dougie. 'Stay there and I'll edge a little closer, see if I can see him better.'

'Be careful,' he mouthed, but I simply shrugged.

'You're the one who needs to be careful, remember? Stay put, and stay silent.'

I edged a little further down the platform towards the man. I hadn't seen him when we'd entered the station earlier. Had he been there all along, hidden in the darkness as Dougie was now, invisible to us as my friend sought somewhere to hide? Or had he entered the station since we'd found a hiding place, choosing this spot on the bench?

The coat he wore was long and black, riding down to just above his knees. His stick-thin legs were covered by thread-bare trousers, while his worn leather boots had seen better days. A filthy scarf was tied about his throat, trailing down on to the bench beside him. A long staff, not dissimilar to a punting pole, rested against the wall behind him, its tip hidden in the eaves of the station house. His attire was peculiar enough, but it was the stovepipe hat that took me by surprise, the black felt tilted forward, rim obscuring his face.

I had to wonder, perhaps he was one of fairground workers, sneaking off for a sly smoke or catching a bit of shut-eye? Either way, this meant the coast was clear for my mate. I looked over my shoulder and called back to him.

'It isn't one of Vinnie's cronies, Dougie. You can come out! He's an Abraham Lincoln lookey-likey! Nothing to be worried about!'

I turned back to the man who was dozing on the bench in time to see him raise a bony finger to the rim of his hat. He pushed it back, sitting slowly upright as if hauled forward on invisible ropes. He rose to his feet, like a puppet on a string, wavering where he stood, face still shrouded by shadows.

'I've got a bad feeling about this,' I whispered as he swivelled his head my way.

Directly my way.

The old lamps that dotted the station suddenly sprang into life, one after another, starting at the far end of the platform and flaring like fireballs. Those lamps had been there since Time was a lad, and I couldn't recall a single occasion they'd ever worked. Hell, I don't think they even had bulbs in them! The tip of the pole roared into life, white flames dancing over the dirty bricks of the station house. The last lights to burst into being were those in the crooked man's eyes as he levelled his hideous gaze upon me.

'It's the Lamplighter's ghost!' screamed Dougie, briefly stirring me from my paralysed state.

I staggered back clumsily, suddenly feeling terribly exposed and vulnerable before the phantom. The same fear that had gripped Dougie and I when we'd first encountered Phyllis was there again, gripping both our hearts as the Lamplighter approached. He snatched the flaming pole up, swinging it like a scythe in one hand while his other reached forward, skeletal fingers outstretched. The monstrous eyes continued to burn, bright and furious in his wizened black skull, hungry as he tottered toward us on spindly legs.

'Move, Will!' shouted Dougie. My friend had found his feet now, but I was terrified. I was dying all over again.

'I don't know who you are, old man, but we've got no business with you,' I blabbed, stumbling slowly back to Dougie – too slowly – my legs turning to jelly. I was vaguely aware of the sound of the train, distant but drawing closer, but I couldn't draw my eyes away from the ghost.

'Run, Will!' Again, from Dougie, but I was deaf to his cries, helpless before the Lamplighter.

'But I have business with you,' he hissed, a cracked black tongue scraping across dried-up, ruined lips. His finger now pointed straight at me. 'A soul as bright as yours, child, would make a most marvellous feast on this cold, cruel night.'

It was *me* he wanted. Not Dougie, not my living, breathing friend. I was the one he could feed upon!

The Lamplighter came forward, a grotesque stick-man, his heels clicking as they found the paved surface of the platform. My throat remained constricted, the phantom squeezing his fist now as if it were buried in my chest, clenched about my heart. The leathery face seemed to crack as a grin spread across it, almost splitting his head in two, his desiccated mouth gaping open as he descended upon me.

I was there one moment, gone the next. It felt like I'd been yanked through the air by a tether, lassoed and whipped away from the Lamplighter before he could get his claws – and teeth – into me. I flew through the air across the tracks, my body passing through the speeding express train as it thundered past the station platform without stopping. Carriages and commuters passed through my spectral form before I emerged on the other side on to the opposite platform.

Dougie had dashed across the footbridge over the tracks, not waiting for me, hoping that our connection would haul me clear before the Lamplighter could harm me. His gamble had done the trick. My friend kept running, exiting the station from the opposite platform, heading back towards the living world and away from the apparition. I looked back as we ran, the lights blinking out on the platform, the ghost disappearing into the darkness.

Each of us emerged on to the road, Dougie almost running headlong into the passing traffic. He collapsed on to the pavement, me by his side, one living, one dead, each of us struggling to compose ourselves. The music of the fairground was welcome to our ears as we tried to smile at one another.

'The next time I need to get to town, I think I'll catch the bus,' gasped Dougie, mopping his brow with the sleeve of his jumper. 'I've always hated trains.'

TWENTY-THREE

Sorrow and Snow

It snowed overnight. This wasn't the smattering that we usually got, a fleeting sneeze of frost from God's left nostril. This was heavier than at any time I could remember. A bit of slush mid-February was the most we could expect, gone within a matter of days. Over the course of that one night we appeared to get hit with ten years' worth of snow, the grim streets transformed into a winter wonderland. It didn't matter that Warrington was surrounded by factories, chimney stacks and power plants: it could've been Santa's backyard. The world was beautiful again, and I missed it more than ever.

In the history of low profiles, Dougie had reached new depths. Our encounter with the demon Lamplighter was really the least of his worries. His antics at the fair on Danger Night had put him top of the school gossip columns the following day. Where was the kid who had not only stood up to Vinnie Savage but also clocked him one? Sure, he hadn't punched him – that had been my doing – but to all intents and purposes it had appeared that way. The whispering campaign had raced around the school like wildfire: Savage *wasn't* indestructible. He could be harmed by mortal man, better still, by *nerds*. If this led to the silent legion of put-upon geeks in our school making a stand against the bullying minority, then it was something Dougie could be proud of. Not that he could see that at present. He was too busy keeping his head down, avoiding the limelight as well as the eyes and ears of Savage's mates. He was hiding in the library.

Of all the rooms within the school, there was one that provided sanctuary against the idiot muscle-heads like Savage. Any bully stepping foot over the library threshold could expect to burn up quicker than a vampire at a picnic. Dougie's day had been spent flitting from classroom to library, dodging the masses and the steady fall of snow. The fact that his trademark parka was now in the possession of Stu Singer meant that the bomber jacket and bobble hat he wore instead allowed him to move incognito, few people recognising him as the legendary Hero of Danger Night. OK, so that wasn't what they were calling him. That was what I'd nicknamed him. I say nickname: I was teasing, obviously.

'They're writing ballads about you in the music room,' said Andy, from where he sat in front of the computer monitor. 'Admittedly it's a bit screechy when played on recorders, but the sentiment's there.'

'Any sign of Stu?' asked Dougie, ignoring Andy's mocking.

'Last seen accepting dares from Year Sevens to sneak on to the roof of Upper School,' replied our friend with a roll of his eyes.

'Always showing off,' I said. 'He hasn't the brains he was born with.'

'You're not wrong,' Dougie said.

Stu's penchant for doing random acts of stupidity was going to get him into trouble one of these days. It was the price he paid for being so frighteningly bright: his words, not mine. Stu was a *really* clever kid, Mensa level of smarts, but for all that intelligence he had zero common sense. It appeared wisdom didn't always come with the territory for the gifted and talented.

'You talking to Will again?' said Andy in answer to Dougie's last remark.

'Sorry,' he replied. 'I forget myself sometimes. Don't feel I have to hide anything when you or Stu are with me.'

'That's very sweet,' Andy said, glancing up from the computer. 'You'll be expressing your undying love for me next, I know it.'

Andy was now up to speed on all that had happened at the House. He'd listened in rapt fascination as Dougie had recounted the series of events that had first led us and then taken us back to the House. The more macabre the better with Andy. The Lamplighter had got him *really* excited. He went so far as asking if we'd take him back to the station to try and encounter the phantom again. That suggestion had been poo-pooed in quite dramatic fashion by Dougie, and I was in no hurry to ever step foot on the platform again. Andy had then set to work.

Although Dungeons and Dragons was his first love, technology was his second, and he was a wizard with computers. Armed with what information we had, he'd spent the last half hour researching the House's past, and in particular the story behind Phyllis Carrington.

'What have you discovered?' asked Dougie, leaning over Andy's shoulder as he brought up a series of open windows on the screen.

'Red Brook House was built in 1856, originally opening its doors as a primary school for boys and girls, becoming a senior school after the Second World War. By the time the Sixties rocked up and there'd been a population boom, it was struggling to handle the greater number of children, only able to accommodate two classes for each school year. It was closed in 1966, as Brooklands High opened.'

'So it's been closed for almost fifty years?' I said. 'Sounds like our maths was spot on with Phyllis, then.'

'What have you discovered about the girl?' said Dougie as Andy brought up another window. 'How did she die?'

'That's just the thing,' shrugged Andy. 'I've searched the old documents that local government keep on file, including news stories from yesteryear. There's no record of a girl named Phyllis Carrington ever dying.'

'So she never existed?'

'That's not what I said,' grinned Andy. 'She existed all right, but she went *missing*. She vanished in December, 1964.'

I joined Dougie, reading over our friend's shoulder as he brought up scanned clippings from old newspapers.

'She wasn't found,' Andy continued. 'One of those mysteries that was never resolved.' He clicked the windows, reducing them one after another.

'Whoa!' I said. 'That page he just got rid of!'

'Hang on, Andy,' said Dougie. 'Bring that page back up from a moment ago.'

Andy backed up, restoring the pages on to the monitor. 'This one? Or this?'

'That's it!' I said as a local history website appeared on the screen.

Dougie stopped Andy clicking on anything else. All three of us craned forward, making a closer examination of the page.

'What am I looking for?' asked Andy.

The menu bar along the top of the page included links to all manner of local historical interest: industry, famous figures, sporting achievements and the like. I pointed at the screen and Dougie followed me, tapping at one particular link so that Andy could highlight it. He clicked on education and another window appeared.

'I'm ahead of you,' he said as a list of years appeared. He clicked on nineteen sixty-four, which brought up the titles of a number of schools. There was Red Brook House. One more click and six thumbnail photographs appeared.

'Open all and open sesame,' said Andy, clicking on the lot of them.

'She was thirteen when she died,' said Dougie as the senior year photos popped up.

'The second year seniors,' I said. 'Their equivalent of Year Eight.'

Dougie pointed, Andy clicked. The screen was filled with a faded sepia photograph of around sixty children, sat in three rows, each higher than the next. Girls sat on the lower bench, with boys at the back and a mixture in the middle. We each scoured the image, but it was my eyes that found her first, a fraction of a second quicker than Dougie's as he pointed Phyllis out for Andy.

There she was, the cute, ponytailed girl with bows in her

pale hair, front row, third in from the left. Monotone though the photo was, I was in no doubt as to the colour of those ribbons. The names of each child were printed at the base of the photograph, barely legible. Dougie squinted as he read out the name from the front row, third along.

'P. Carrington.'

My heart skipped a beat, seeing the ghost girl there on the screen, as she was in life. The empathy I already felt for her was magnified, seeing her innocent smile months, weeks, perhaps even days before her terrible fate occurred. My eyes drifted across the crowd of children, my mind imagining the various friendships, acquaintances or indeed rivalries Phyllis might have had with those kids. There was a Lucy Carpenter amongst their number, and a Vinnie Savage no doubt. *Which one would've been me?* I wondered, staring at the boys who stood to attention along the back row. I gasped.

'Back row, far right,' I said, as Dougie read out the name.

'E. Borley.'

He looked back to the rakish figure at the back of the group, the familiar hook nose making him instantly recognisable. The caretaker's cold, dark eyes stared out of the screen at us, deep into our very souls. Dougie gulped and glanced at me.

'Crap,' added Andy, succinctly.

Our shocked stupor was broken by a commotion outdoors.

Dougie looked out of the window and could see a crowd had gathered in the playground. There must have been a hundred kids, huddling together in the snow next to the Upper School building.

'What's going on?' I asked.

'Looks like a fight, perhaps?' said Dougie.

Andy stood and cranked open the library window to shout at one of the Year Sevens who was rushing past.

'What's happened?'

'That big lad who dared to climb on to the Upper School roof,' said the kid excitedly, his face a mixture of horror and morbid excitement. 'He's only gone and jumped, hasn't he.'

Andy and Dougie didn't wait around, grabbing their jackets and bags as they legged it for the door. I floated along beside them, fearing what awaited us when we got to the scene of the fall, a blizzard of snow hitting us as we dashed outdoors. I always said his stupidity would be the death of Stu. I hadn't suspected this might be that day.

TWENTY-FOUR

Accident and Emergency

It was the last place I'd expected to return to. I thought after my sudden departure from the living world I was done with the General Hospital, but here I was back, only this time with Dougie and on account of another poor fool. Actually, scratch that. I hadn't been foolish. I couldn't have foreseen what would happen to me on the awful night of my death. Nobody had made Stu climb on to the top of the Upper School. Nobody had bent his arm, forced him to scramble on to an icy rooftop three storeys high. He could have avoided the terrible fate that had followed, but a brain-fart of colossal proportions had prevented common sense from kicking in. I mean, what harm could possibly come to anyone on top of a lofty, snow-covered building in blizzard conditions?

By the time Dougie and I arrived at the hospital, the night

was already drawing in. Dougie had grabbed a bus into Warrington straight after school, travel by rail still an impossibility thanks to the train station's resident soul-devouring ghost. We had journeyed in shocked silence, wondering what awaited us. As we walked up to the entrance to A&E, I felt a sickening dread rising in the pit of my stomach. The blue lights on ambulances flashed nearby, casting their pale, revolving glow on to the hospital's grim walls. Here was the building where I'd put together my terrible conundrum. This was where I'd realised I was dead, returned as a ghost. I stopped walking, hovering in the air outside the sliding doors as paramedics and patients rushed in and out. Dougie stood to one side, dragging me with him.

'Are you OK, Will?'

'I'm just a bit . . . apprehensive.'

'Understandable, mate, under the circumstances.'

Neither of us knew how bad things might be for Stu. By the time we'd arrived at the scene of his fall, a dozen teachers had already formed a ring around him, while others proceeded to shoo students away. Dougie had tried to squeeze through to see better, but had found his path blocked. I faced no such obstacle. I drifted forward, phasing through geography teacher Mr Hopwood, until I stood over my stricken friend. Mrs Jolly, the school nurse, crouched beside Stu, leaning over him, talking to him, seeing if she could stir a response from him. He lay spreadeagled on his back, limbs out at every angle, buried deep in the snow. As Dougie was forced away from the scene, I was drawn back with him, away from Stu's motionless body. The remainder of the day had been spent worrying about what condition he was in, as an ambulance arrived and whisked him hurriedly away.

'Do you think ... if anything happens to Stu ...?' said Dougie.

'What? That he'll come back like me? I don't know. I'm not sure how the whole ghostly gubbins works, mate. Think of Phyllis. Who knows what her story is?'

'It's fair to say Borley's at the heart of it,' said Dougie. 'We need to see her again. Find out—'

His words were cut short as he stared slack-jawed into the building. I turned to see what had silenced him.

'You seeing him too?' he asked, and I nodded.

A man in his early thirties, wreathed in a pale light, was walking through the A&E lobby, clad in an old-fashioned military uniform. He turned our way as he strode confidently by, coming to a halt between the sliding doors. Rank insignia adorned his left breast pocket, marking him as an officer. He smiled at us both before sending his hand to his brow in an elegant salute. Then he was on his way again, disappearing through the wall at the end of the reception area.

'OK,' I said with a whisper. 'That was interesting. Make a note in your little black book, Dougie: return to hospital and have a chat with "the Major" at some point in near future.'

'So long as he's the nice kind of ghost as opposed to another Lamplighter, eh? Did you not see him last time you were here?' he asked as we entered the building, staring at the wall that the old soldier had disappeared through.

'I was kind of preoccupied, chum, what with having just died and all that fun and nonsense. There could've been all manner of spooks walking around that night and I wouldn't have noticed. That said, it seems Phyllis was right: you *are* tuned in to some ghostly wavelength now. Whatever I'm seeing, you're getting it too.'

Dougie stepped up to the receptionist.

'Hiya, I've come to see my mate—'

'Have you taken a ticket?'

'Sorry?'

'Have you taken a ticket?'

'I just want to check up on—'

'You need to take a ticket.'

'Can't you just check—'

'Take a ticket.'

With a sigh, Dougie stepped to one side and took a stub from the machine. It was a dozen shy of the number on the readout above the receptionist's head.

'Can't be chewed waiting for the honour of speaking with that old dragon again,' said Dougie, screwing up the ticket and chucking it into a waste bin. 'Let's see what we can find out for ourselves.'

Dougie hopped over to a water fountain and bent his neck to rub water into his eyes.

'What on earth are you doing?' I asked, but he paid me no attention.

Backing out of the sliding doors, we spied a lady paramedic and her driver sat on the back step of their ambulance, supping plastic beakers of tea. The woman looked up as Dougie approached.

'You all right, son?' she asked.

'I'm looking for my brother,' he sniffed, wiping the faux tears from his eyes. 'He was brought in this afternoon, had fallen from the school roof.'

'Oh, you poor love,' she said, placing the cup on the step and rising to give him a hug. 'You're in a right state. I know who you're on about, we were the responders. Tom, stay here and keep an eye on my brew. I'll be back in a mo. You can come with me.'

She took Dougie by the hand and led him back indoors, my mate throwing me a wink as she set off through the A&E. Leading us to a lift at the back of the Casualty department, we were soon up on the second floor and travelling down a long corridor, passing wards on either side. The paramedic made small talk with Dougie, trying to sound positive as we drew ever closer to our destination.

'Your dad's the Reverend Singer, isn't he? Lovely fella. He's here already,' she said.

'He is?' asked Dougie, suddenly worried that his cover would be blown at any second.

'I'm told he's helping the police answer some questions at the moment, back downstairs. Wouldn't you prefer I take you straight to them?'

'I'd rather see my brother first,' said Dougie, chancing a reply.

'Try not to worry, love,' she said, squeezing his hand tightly. 'Try not to worry.'

I could tell by the way she was speaking and her body language that whatever had happened to Stu had been pretty grim. The sick feeling in my belly returned, twice as bad as before, my guts in knots. Two large, automatic doors stood at the end of the corridor, adorned with badly illustrated paintings of Disney characters. After a brief chat through the intercom, the doors opened and we walked in.

'Sit yourself there, lovely,' said the paramedic, pointing Dougie to the waiting area. 'I'll go see what I can find out for you. Back in a mo.'

With the ambulance worker gone, there was no need to

hang around. Dougie joined me as we looked down the corridors that made up the ward. We set off, passing rooms where kids of all ages lay in beds, some with arms or legs in plaster, raised from their mattresses, others hidden beneath their sheets, feeling sorry for themselves. It quickly became apparent that he wasn't on one of the open wards. The only other place he could be was in a side room.

Moving quickly down the corridor that housed the private rooms, I dipped my head through each door. After three peek-and-see head-bobs I found him. The blinds were down over the windows in the room, including over the panel in the door. Stu lay on a bed covered in pristine white sheets, hooked up to all manner of medical paraphernalia. I popped back into the corridor and beckoned Dougie, who slipped into the room as quickly as he could.

We stood over Stu's body on the bed. A collar was fastened firmly around his neck, keeping it motionless. His right leg and arm were both in plaster, suspended from the ceiling by a network of cables and pulleys. The *pings*, *bleeps* and *beeps* of the machines provided an odd electrical chorus, as we watched Stu's chest slowly rise and fall.

'Thank God,' I said, relieved that I wasn't encountering a ghostly incarnation of my mate in the room.

'Stupid sod,' muttered Dougie, shaking his head.

'Takes one . . . to know one . . .' wheezed Stu, his eyes still

187

closed. Dougie and I both jumped to hear him speak, the revelation met with shock and joy.

'What were you thinking, daft arse?' asked Dougie, reaching out and taking Stu's left hand in his own. He gave our friend's palm a squeeze.

'Have you got Will with you, then?'

'He's right here,' grinned Dougie.

Stu opened his bloodshot eyes and glanced my way, guessing my whereabouts. 'Tell him he'll have to wait. I'm not ready for that reunion just yet.'

'He's smiling at that,' said Dougie, and he wasn't lying. A tear rolled down my cheek, I was so happy to see Stu was alive. 'How bad is it?'

'Arm and leg broken, and they're waiting for test results on my back,' Stu grimaced. 'Reckon they'll be putting plates and rods and stuff in there. I'll be more machine than man when I'm done.'

'More muppet than man,' I said.

'You do realise what a complete member you were, climbing on to the roof when it was covered in snow?' said Dougie, his voice serious now. 'I get that you like showing off, but that sounded like a death wish.'

'I only peeked over the edge, Dougie, I swear,' said Stu with a grunt. 'I'm not that daft that I'd risk my life. I had hold of the air conditioning vents up there, I wasn't going to fall.'

'Yet you did fall, Stu,' corrected Dougie. 'And it's only by blind luck and a very healthy blanket of snow that you're still alive.'

'You ain't listening,' said Stu. 'Your coat's over there, pal. You can have it back, whatever condition it's in.'

His clothes were piled up on a chair beside the bed. There was Dougie's parka, the green jacket draped over its back. My mate picked it up, shaking it out, droplets of meltwater from the snow flicked across the floor.

'What the hell did you do to it?'

The distinctive hood was gone, torn free, the padding sprouting out in tufts from the ripped material.

'Like I said, you haven't been listening,' spluttered Stu. 'I didn't do that to the jacket. It happened on top of the Upper School. He tore it!'

'Who tore it off?' asked Dougie as I felt a chill seize my heart.

Stu's red eyes were wide now.

'Whoever pushed me off the roof.'

TWENTY-FIVE

Rooftops and Revelations

With all eyes on the hospital and the fortunes of an injured daredevil, Brooklands High was quiet as a crypt, entombed in snow. Dougie and I stared at the sprawling expanse of buildings from the wrong side of the gates, my friend having just hauled himself over the railings. Inevitably our gaze lingered upon the top of the science block, scene of Big Stu's awful accident. Only it wasn't an accident, was it? Our friend reckoned he'd been shoved, his plummet intentional at the hands of another. And that would-be-killer was still out there. Perhaps he'd killed before?

Dougie crept across the car park, sidling along the low wall that ran along its edge, sticking to the shadows as he covered the distance to the buildings. His old parka was back on – minus the hood – while the bobble on his woolly hat shook with every step. I sensed two emotions rolling off him as I drifted along at his side: fear and anger. Fear that he might get caught, and anger that someone might have tried to harm our friend. It was too much of a coincidence that Stu was wearing that coat when he was pushed from the rooftop. Dougie had been the target, and it scared him witless.

One solitary light shone from the entire school, the warm yellow glow from the headmaster's office illuminating the snow that was banked up outside. For Goodman to stay late wasn't unusual. For him to stay late on this particular night was testament to his guilt that such a terrible thing should happen to one of his pupils – a child in his care – on his watch.

'Keep your eyes open,' Dougie said as he placed his gloved hands either side of the drainpipe that led to the roof of the Lower School. An expansive, single-floor building, Borley's office was in the heart of this maze of classrooms. Up Dougie went, using bricks and brackets as foot and handholds. Reaching up he took hold of the lead flashing on the roof, hauling himself the remaining distance until his belly slid over the edge. The snow crunched beneath his gut as he rolled forward, his legs swinging after him.

Looking up at the stars overhead, Dougie took a moment to compose himself, his breath clouding in front of him before dissipating.

'Another cold one,' I said as he struggled to his feet. 'You put your thermal long johns on?'

'Yes. Thanks for your concern, Mother,' he said as he trudged through the virgin snow along the rooftop. 'I hope Stu comes through this. I can't help but feel responsible for what's happened to him.'

'Don't beat yourself up. It was Stu who chose to climb up there like a lunatic in the first place. Admittedly he didn't choose to swan dive off the roof, but he was daft to be up there.'

'He'd never have been pushed if he wasn't wearing my jacket.'

I had nothing to say about that. Dougie was right. It was a case of mistaken identity that had sent Stu over the edge. If he hadn't been wearing the green parka he'd probably still be goofing around like the grade-A clown he was.

We crept across the rooftops, clambering over low walls, stepping around air conditioners and hurdling pipes and gutters. We were thankful for the clear sky: bitterly cold as it was, it afforded us a great view of the school and where we were heading.

'It should be here,' I said, the floor crunching beneath Dougie's feet. 'Hang on, fella.'

Walking in any direction was a relatively easy notion for me, following the same principles that were second nature to me in life. Although I didn't exist in the living world, I instinctively knew how to move through it, the memory of it deeply ingrained in my psyche. Stepping through a wall had taken some getting used to, but it was simply an extension of walking forward. To force myself down, through the floor, felt deeply unnatural, and not a small bit sickening, but it had to be done. I tipped my body and directed my mind and spirit through the ground, my body sinking like a diver might in a pool. I slipped beneath the snow-covered floor, through the bitumen- and felt-coated roof and timbers, until I materialised in Borley's office.

I took a quick look around the dark room, a faint light within from the snow-covered skylight above. Popping skyward once more I took a moment to gather my bearings. I wagged my finger at a spot a few feet away.

'There,' I said. 'A skylight.'

Quickly, Dougie was on his knees, scooping the ice to one side, clawing at it with his gloves. I stood to one side, looking around frantically, feeling very much like the accomplice in some terrible crime. Was it really a crime, though? We knew what we were doing was righteous. There had to be a clue within Borley's office that connected him to not only Phyllis' death in the House, but also the attempted murder of our friend, Stu.

The domed perspex sheet was now visible, Dougie scraping

the snow away from around its edge. He felt around, trying to find a way in. Reaching into the pocket of his parka, he whipped out a long, flathead screwdriver, wiggling it under the rubber seal and working it against the latch. Sawing it back and forth, he ripped his gloves off as he struggled for traction. He grunted as he forced the screwdriver to its limit, eyes bulging, until the latch inside suddenly popped. The skylight gave, rattling in its bracket as more snow was shaken loose from its sloping summit. Easing his fingers beneath the rim, Dougie pulled hard, the window suddenly groaning as it extended to its limit, a metal arm holding it open. There was a gap of about a foot that could be navigated through. It was going to be a squeeze.

'I know it's your lucky jacket and you've only just got it back, but you're gonna have to take the parka off, D,' I said. 'There's no way you'll fit through there with that on.'

Begrudgingly he shook it off, taking the mini torch out of one of its deep pockets.

'How far to the floor?'

'About ten feet,' I replied.

'Joy. How will I get back up?'

'He's got a swivel chair down there, plus there's a filing cabinet to the side of the skylight. You'll be OK, I reckon.'

'You reckon?' he said incredulously. 'Oh, to share your optimism!'

'Stop gassing, let's get on with it. Some of us have got homes to go to!'

'Yeah, mine!' he replied before popping his torch into his mouth, switching it on and wiggling down through the open skylight.

His landing would've looked cool and catlike if it hadn't been for the crusty layer of snow on the soles of his boots. His feet shot out from beneath him, sending him thumping on to his rump with a yowl.

'Shut it!' I said. 'Goodman is in his office, remember?'

I was already looking around the office as my mate righted himself. I took a glance out of the wire-meshed window that opened out on to the pitch-dark Lower School corridor. A large cork board filled one wall, covered in a multitude of Post-its, notes, sheets of paper and memos. A big old oak desk dominated the room, littered with screws, nails, tools and trays. The leatherette top was scored and slashed, peeling around the edges and curling at the corners. A giant pile of manuals was stacked at the back, topped by a filthy, tea-stained mug.

Instantly Dougie was into the filing cabinets while I scoured the notice board. It was surprisingly light in the office now with the window clear and the stars lighting the room, plus the occasional sweeping arc of Dougie's torch provided added illumination too. There were phone numbers with names alongside them pinned to the cork, none of them sending my Spidey sense tingling. Instruction pamphlets sat alongside menus for takeaway delivery firms and the like. After I'd been over the board twice I turned to see how Dougie was getting on, my friend now on the final drawer of the filing cabinet.

'Nothing here, mate,' he said. 'Which leaves us with the desk. There won't be anything there, will there? If he does have any mementos, he probably keeps them at home like any good serial killer.'

It was a glib, throwaway comment, inspired by the many horror movies we'd seen, but he wasn't too far off the mark. Borley was a dangerous man. Who knew what he was capable of?

The side drawers of the desk opened easily, revealing more of the same clutter within. Dougie sifted through it all, looking for a clue that might help us catch Borley out. There was nothing. Fed up, Dougie collapsed into the chair and spun about.

'Nothing. What a waste of time.'

'Not entirely,' I said. 'We've ruled out his office. Next thing to do is try his home.'

'You're having a laugh, dude! I'm not breaking into his house, wherever it is. This is bad enough, sneaking into the school. I'll be expelled if I get caught here. No way, Will. I'm done with this.'

He reached out and started picking at the leatherette.

'Dougie, we're so close, mate.'

'So close to what? Stu nearly died today! What next?'

He was right. We were walking a line that was growing more dangerous by the second. I shrugged and nodded as Dougie suddenly stopped scratching at the desk's surface.

'Hang about,' he said, snatching his torch and throwing the light below the desktop's rim. 'There's another drawer here, set back.'

I crouched and looked. Sure enough there was. 'It's a stationery drawer. For pens, paper and all that.'

Dougie tried to feel for a handle but found none. He squinted. 'There's a keyhole here.' He jabbed his screwdriver into it, trying to prise it open.

'Locked?' I asked, as Dougie nodded. 'What on earth are you hiding, Mr Borley?'

My friend moved the tool round to the drawer's edge and hammered it into the thin gap with the palm of his hand. Then he gave it a whack. The drawer popped open on a spring, Dougie's fingertips awaiting it as it extended forward over his lap.

While the top of the desk was in utter ruination, the interior of the stationery drawer was in immaculate condition. Lined in green baize, there was a pile of neatly stacked newspaper cuttings. A glance at the top article told us all we needed to know. It was dated the nineteenth of December, 1964, and was about the disappearance of one Phyllis Carrington. Her face was there, a sweet family portrait with her head dipped to one side, blonde pigtails bobbing. There was Phyllis, staring back at us. And there was the school photo – an original though – the one we'd found online with Andy. Every cutting, every article: each was about the disappearance of our ghostly friend, a scrapbook of horror.

The cuttings weren't the most shocking thing though. I tried to find the words, to tell Dougie what we'd discovered, but I didn't need to. His trembling fingers brushed the long red ribbon that had bound the newspaper articles together, tied neatly in an elegant bow.

'We need to get out of here,' I whispered. 'Now.'

Dougie made to pick up the bundle.

'No,' I said. 'We need to leave it here. If we take them, it's not proof at all as to his involvement. The clippings and the ribbon: they need to be found here by an authority figure.'

'Who, then?'

'I don't know,' I hissed, exasperated. 'But we need to leave this room as we found it. Come on. Get it closed. We should put our heads together and trap Borley red-handed.'

TWENTY-SIX

Blues and Twos

When the police cars descended upon our high school the next day, it was fair to say Dougie and I shared feelings of absolute unadulterated delight. Here was the reward for our sleuthing and dogged determination. From the first moment we'd spied him at the House we knew something was awry. As time went on, he'd revealed himself to be irrevocably connected with Phyllis Carrington's abduction and death. Perhaps now, with the police questioning him, they might get to the bottom of what had happened to our poor friend in the Sixties. This was our moment of triumph and, sitting on the bench by the school gates, we'd got ringside seats to enjoy it. In true Scooby-Doo style, he would've gotten away with it if it wasn't for us pesky kids.

Andy Vaughn sat on one side of Dougie, while I attempted an approximation of chilling out on the other side of him. This is incredibly hard to do when one considers that my buttocks carry all the weight of an air biscuit, but still, I wanted to be by my best mate's side when they hauled Borley out of the school in handcuffs.

'All credit to you chaps,' said Andy, who'd helped us put the finishing touches to our case. 'I can't quite believe you've done it. That's some going. You really think those printouts will have helped?'

'Deffo,' said Dougie. 'Those documents, alongside our letter, will be what stirred Goodman into calling the rozzers. He wouldn't have picked up the phone without them, I reckon.'

First thing that morning, at stupid o'clock, Andy had been rudely awakened by Dougie. Sidestepping Mrs Vaughn's protestations, he'd sloped up to Andy's bedroom and fired up the laptop. Andy had very kindly printed off the various documents about Phyllis' disappearance from the local history website, including newspaper stories and those old school photos. Alongside a carefully worded letter from us that spelled out what Borley had been up to, and how he'd inevitably been the one responsible for the attempted murder of Stu Singer, it had proved a damning dossier. Delivered in a brown, A4 envelope, Dougie had declared he'd felt like a cold war spy when he slid the folder under Mr Goodman's office door first thing in the morning.

'You're sure Goodman didn't see you deliver the letter this morning?' asked Andy.

'Nah, he rocked up after we'd done it, his car wasn't in the car park.'

'He's going to know it was from you anyway, matey,' I said. 'You don't have to be Sherlock to work that out. Goodman knows you were snooping around the House, remember?'

'Well,' said Dougie with a triumphant sigh. 'I don't feel the need to get involved now. Let the professionals run with it from here. Doesn't matter if Goodman knows it's me behind the package, it's the cops who can take care of the rest now. I'm glad to be shot of the terrible business.'

The letter hadn't gone so far as saying what exactly was in the desk, or indeed that Borley's desk held the key to the old crime, but we'd laid a series of subtle breadcrumbs that Goodman – and in turn the police – would be able to follow. We were at pains to make it clear that we hadn't been *into* the office – that would have weakened our case immeasurably. Once they got into the office, they were bound to turn it over searching for the incriminating evidence, and the bundle of letters with the big red ribbon would finally, fantastically reveal themselves to them. The discovery would be all down to Mr Goodman. He was welcome to the publicity that would no doubt follow. The last thing Dougie craved was the limelight. He just wanted his life to go back to normal. Well, as normal as it can be when your best friend's a ghost.

'Does this mean you get to go and tell Phyllis the good news?' asked Andy.

'I guess it does,' smiled Dougie. 'I'll probably leave that honour to Will though. She's his girlfriend after all.'

'Ouch,' I said as deadpan as I could muster. 'My sides. Please. They're splitting. Incredible, even when I'm dead you can find the time to tease me about talking to girls. Heaven help you the day *you* finally snare yourself a girlfriend. And heaven help her for that matter.'

I rolled my eyes as Dougie elbowed Andy, pointing at me (that is, the thin air beside him).

'I've ticked him off with that,' he said. He slapped his leg tearfully, guffawing at his own joke. It was then my turn to laugh as he doubled up in pain, holding his thigh where he'd cut it at the House.

'Actually,' said Andy, ignoring how Dougie's tears had shifted suddenly from ones of hilarity to discomfort. 'Do you reckon I can come along when you next go to see her?'

Dougie gradually composed himself and sucked his teeth. 'I don't know about that, Andy. Form tells us that Phyllis doesn't play well with others, certainly not on first meeting. Let us run it by her first?'

Andy nodded while I spoke up, for Dougie's ears only. 'You're also forgetting the fact that it's unlikely he'll see anything anyhow. He can't see me, after all. The only reason *you* can see her is that you've hooked into my ghostly vibes somehow, nicking my spooky broadband.'

Dougie nodded to me and winked to Andy, slowly and gently massaging the life back into his injured thigh. He'd aggravated the injury last night as he'd struggled out of the skylight, causing it to open again and bleed through his jeans, but it had been worth it. We turned back to the school office as the front doors opened and one of the uniformed policemen stepped out, speaking into his radio. He had a see-through zip-lock evidence bag crooked under his arm. From this distance it was hard to tell what was inside, but I thought I saw a flash of dark green before he placed it inside his coat. I glanced toward the squad car that was parked at the front of the school, an officer waiting expectantly by an open back door.

'Things are beginning to get interesting,' said Andy, sitting up straight as two plain-clothes officers stepped out of the school, leading Mr Borley between them. A jacket had been thrown over his wrists, no doubt hiding the handcuffs beneath. The old caretaker's head was dipped low as he left the office, avoiding eye contact with the others gathered there. The teachers fell silent as he walked through them, their banter halting when faced by the sight of Borley's shameful promenade.

I could feel my chest swelling with pride as he was marched ever closer to us. They'd have to walk him past the bench we were sat on as they exited the gates. He glanced at us as they passed. As much as I hated the old man for all he'd done, I was struck by the sadness in his eyes. He was led away, broken, and placed into the back of the squad car. The blue lights flashed, the siren *whooped* once, and they were off, heading down the road in the direction of town and the main police headquarters.

The crowd of teachers and support staff had followed, all standing nearby as the car disappeared out of sight. Mrs Jolly was closest to us, the bubbly nurse coming over to tell the boys to get inside.

'It's freezing out here,' she said. 'You'll catch your death!'

'Why've they taken Mr Borley away, miss?' asked Andy, knowingly.

'He's done something very bad, it appears,' she said, wide-eyed. 'The police want to talk to him about what happened to Stuart Singer. There, I've already probably said too much!'

'Stu Singer?' said Dougie. 'Why do they want to talk to him about Stu?'

'Because they found something in his office, Hancock,' said Mr Goodman, appearing beside Mrs Jolly as if by magic.

He glowered at the nurse. 'Isn't there somewhere you should be, Mrs Jolly, as opposed to gossiping with pupils?'

'Oh yes, sorry sir,' she said, blushing furiously and suitably admonished as she set off back toward the office, the other teachers alongside her. Goodman had a way about him: the teachers were as intimidated by him as the pupils were! He turned back to Dougie.

'That jacket, lad,' said Goodman. 'The police will be needing that as they build a case against Mr Borley. That's evidence you're wearing.'

Reluctantly, Dougie shook off his parka and was coatless, not for the first time that week.

'Is that what they want him for then, sir? Stu's fall from the Upper School roof?'

'Indeed. Seems Mr Borley's been a very naughty boy.' He leaned in close, his voice a whisper. 'I know it was you, Hancock: the tip-off. Good work, my boy. Now for your own health and sanity you need to step aside and let the police get on with their business. Don't make me sign that letter to the psychiatrist, you hear me?'

Dougie nodded and Goodman gave him a wink.

'Good.'

'What was it they found, sir?' asked Andy, finding his voice before the head at last.

'Evidence, lad,' said Goodman. 'One telltale little thing

that Borley tried to hide. One miserable item that'll put him behind bars where he belongs.'

'Just the one item?' I said, and Dougie heard me. 'It was a big pile of cuttings and the ribbon. *That* was the damning evidence!'

The newspaper bundle was what should point the police in the direction of Phyllis and the House. I began to wonder now what it was the police had taken in the evidence bag.

'What was the evidence they took away, sir?' said Dougie, echoing Andy's earlier question.

'The hood to this jacket, lad,' said Goodman, flinging the torn green garment over his shoulder and setting off back toward the school office as if he were strolling on a sunny summer afternoon.

'You never mentioned the hood,' hissed Andy when Goodman was out of earshot.

'That's because we never *saw* the flaming hood!' said Dougie frantically. 'They *have* to have found the cuttings and the ribbon too. It's the ribbon that ties him to Phyllis! That's where this all began!'

We were off, running through Lower School in the direction of Borley's office. Turning the corner, we spied one of the Year Eleven prefects standing to attention outside the closed door. You'd think he'd been charged with guarding the Ark of the Covenant the way he was standing, chin out, eyes ahead.

A serious soul, but thankfully, easily fooled by the oldest ruse in the book.

'Quick!' said Andy, running up to him and tugging his elbow. 'Madamoiselle Pasquale has fallen over on the ice on Upper School playground! She's hurt her ankle!'

And with that the perfect prefect was off, keen to be the knight in shining armour. The lure of aiding the damsel in distress – on this occasion, the stunningly beautiful French student teacher – was too great to resist. The only thing missing was the Superman cape as he disappeared around the corner and left his post unmanned.

Dougie tried the handle to Borley's office: locked. The pair of us were alarmed now, worried that somehow the police had missed the main clue we'd left for them, the one that implicated the caretaker in the initial crime. I slipped through the door, my heart racing, fear taking hold of me at the prospect of a police oversight. I punched the desk, focusing my anger into the blow. Sure enough, the leatherette top shuddered as the sprung stationery drawer flew open.

It was empty. The evidence was gone. That could mean only one thing: the police had found the evidence and taken it with them. Well, that or somebody else had.

TWENTY-SEVEN

Winners and Losers

It felt weird to be able to walk down the moonlit driveway that led to Red Brook House without fear of being followed by Borley. It had been the longest few days of my life – well, un-life, but you know what I mean – and I was relieved they were finally drawing to a close. A fight in a fairground, an encounter with a wicked ghost, an attempted murder and the capture of a killer. And all before the school had broken up for Christmas! God only knew what awaited Dougie and me in the New Year.

'I wonder,' I said as we strolled triumphantly over the snow-covered gravel toward the red-brick building. 'Do you think Phyllis will be able to move on, now?'

'Why?' replied Dougie breezily. 'Because Borley's been caught? I dunno, mate. Hope so. Still not sure how it works.'

'I'm pretty sure we're here until we solve the circumstances of our untimely deaths. Perhaps she can rest in peace now.'

'That'd be nice.'

I mumbled as we neared the doors to the House, fresh snow beginning to fall.

'I recognise that monosyllabic grunt,' said Dougie. 'What's the matter?'

I shrugged, a little shamefaced. 'I'm going to miss her, is all. We had a connection.'

'You've got a connection with me, regardless of how much I try and shake you off!'

'That's not what I mean. She's the one person – the one and only ghost – that I could talk to about my predicament. We're in the same boat. That's a pretty unique perspective.'

Clambering on to the broken windowsill, Dougie eased his legs round and into the building, carefully avoiding further injury. He landed with a thump as I materialised through the wall by his side.

'Will, you're going to have to let her go, mate. If she gets her chance to move on, you have to encourage her to take it. You can't be selfish on this one. Think about how you'd feel if you had the chance to rest at last?'

'I know, mate,' I said as we set off up the staircase into the House.

Now that Dougie had mentioned it, I afforded myself a

moment to consider what I'd do if my chance came along. Would I take it? Could I?

'She might not even be here,' I said as we reached the second-floor landing and set off down the corridor. 'She could've gone already.'

'Without saying goodbye to her boyfriend?' grinned Dougie wickedly. 'Don't think she'd do that to you, mate.'

Dougie jumped suddenly as a rat scuttled out of the skirting board and across his path, sending him clattering into the wall. I didn't even attempt to hide my smug grin as I continued on ahead.

'That'll learn you,' I said as we turned the corner of Phyllis' classroom and entered.

There she was, standing by the window, looking outside as the snow slowly fell. Her pale hand hovered over the sill, her other one placed in approximation against the glass. She looked our way as we entered, our smiles slipping as we saw her weary face.

'I feel a great sadness,' she whispered. 'And I don't know why.'

'Could it be,' I said, walking through the desks to be beside her, 'that whatever sorrow has haunted you, kept you here all these years, has lifted?'

'I don't know. Surely I'd feel my misery disappear if that were the case?'

'You're feeling *more* unhappy?' asked Dougie, joining us in the moonlight.

'All I know is I feel a weight, like never before, growing all around me,' she said, her hand going to her throat and massaging her ghostly flesh. I reached out and took her other hand in my own, feeling immeasurable comfort in the sensation.

'Can you explain it?' I asked.

'The air feels thin,' she whispered, 'as if I'm being pushed down and crushed, deafened and drowned. Why should that be?'

Could *that* be what I should expect? Was this what it would feel like for me when I finally moved on? A sickening, awful sensation to endure? I squeezed her hand.

'It'll pass, Phyllis, I promise you. Whatever happened to you, so long ago, it's being resolved now at last.'

'He faces justice as we speak,' added Dougie.

My smile was victorious, Dougie's grin mirroring my own. She glanced at the two of us, trying to comprehend what we were telling her.

'Who?'

'We mentioned him to you before, and I recall you wigging out,' I said. 'It's Borley, isn't it? Do you remember him?'

'Eric Borley,' she whispered, looking across to the fireplace. She walked across and knelt on the floor before it, casting her eyes over the eerie shrine of books and candles. 'I remember Eric Borley. He was my ... friend.'

'And it was he who ... was responsible for your death,' I said, stopping short of reminding her that she'd been murdered.

'Eric wouldn't have done that,' she replied, her hand still around her throat. 'Eric was a good lad. You've got him wrong.'

'You're his terrible secret, Phyllis,' I said, crouching beside her. 'Don't you see that? He did something awful, something unimaginable, that left you this way. You might have thought he was your mate, but you got him all wrong. He was a bad lad—'

'He was *not*,' she shouted, angry now, turning on me. 'Don't talk about him that way. These mementos – the candles, my books, my precious things – they're all here because of him. He tends to this shrine. He keeps it safe. He keeps the House safe.'

'Out of *guilt*!' I said.

'Out of *love*!' she replied, shamefully. 'He loved me from afar throughout my life, my mate who played by my side but could never tell me how he truly felt. I've seen him return here, every week, for fifty years, saying his prayers, speaking to my memories, wishing he could've changed what had happened. Wishing he could've *been there* for me.'

'Wishing he hadn't done what he'd done, you mean?' said Dougie.

'He didn't do anything,' she exclaimed. 'I swear, you've got him all wrong. He wasn't with me that night. He was at home, full of the flu.'

'You remember what happened?' I said. 'You seem sure enough that Borley wasn't involved, now.'

'I dunno,' said Dougie. 'He seemed awful guilty. All that business chasing me, coming after me, pushing Stu off the roof: he even keeps one of your ribbons in his desk, you know?'

Phyllis lifted a hand to her pale yellow hair and trailed it through a faded bow.

'He was protecting me, protecting my memory. Eric Borley's a good man. He's my friend.'

'I'm beginning to think we should have gone straight to the police and not Goodman,' said Dougie with a grumble.

I nodded. 'Perhaps taking a back seat at the end there wasn't the best plan of action after all. We need to make sure they have the *full* story, and not just part of it.'

'Goodman?' whispered Phyllis, her voice catching suddenly. She gasped and went pale, even for a ghost.

'What's the matter?' I asked, taking her in my arms.

'I knew a Goodman at school,' she said fearfully. 'A couple of years older than me. His family moved to Warrington from

Yorkshire, I recall. He'd have been about fifteen at the time, I guess. A real loner. Never made any friends. He would follow me. He would watch me . . .'

Her eyes were wide as saucers, her face frozen with terror. 'He was a bad lad.'

The front doors to Red Brook House slammed shut, quickly followed by heavy thumping footsteps on the staircase, rising ever higher.

'Oh crap,' whispered Dougie. 'What have we done?'

TWENTY-EIGHT

Bricks and Bones

Stepping across the threshold, one heavy black boot followed another as Mr Goodman slowly entered the classroom. He had a sack over his shoulder, a large hessian affair that clunked and clicked with every movement. Placing it on the floor, he pulled out the old-fashioned Davy lamp from his office and placed it on to a desk. Removing a lighter from his pocket he gave it a deft flick, passing the flame on to the lantern's wick. Adjusting the lamp, he allowed its glow to illuminate the classroom, bathing the cold chamber in a flickering, golden light. He re-pocketed the lighter, the metal casing catching Borley's large keyring where it hung from his belt. Standing upright, Goodman sighed and looked around the room, soaking in the atmosphere for a moment.

'Haunted, my eye!' he chuckled.

With the lamp in one hand, he picked the sack up in the other and began to stroll around the room, inspecting the walls. Occasionally he would pause, biting his lip and squinting as he inspected an area of plasterwork. He'd step back and turn toward the front of the class, getting his bearings once more before shaking his head and searching elsewhere.

'What's he doing?' Dougie whispered as silently as he could, his voice masked by the clunking noises from inside the sack. He was hidden behind the fish tank, having luckily been able to manoeuvre it just enough to squeeze into the gap between cabinet and wall. His head and shoulders were covered in dust, dislodged as he'd hurriedly shifted the ancient furniture.

'I've no idea,' I replied, 'but shut up for heaven's sake! If he hears you, you'll be for it!'

'You're still talking!' sniffed Dougie, stifling a sneeze.

'He can't *hear me,*' I replied. 'Keep up, idiot!'

I stood to one side of the fish tank with Phyllis' face turned in to my chest, unable to watch. I could hear her breathing now, wheezing and laboured, as though the proximity of the headmaster was making her worse. Goodman held power over her, even after death. How could we have got it so wrong? Had we really hounded Borley, convinced he was the reason this poor girl had died so long ago? We hadn't even considered anyone else, any other scenario where the caretaker might have been innocent. The killer had been in plain sight all along, listening to Dougie's troubled ramblings, providing counsel when he was low. That was why he wanted us to butt out, why he needed us to stay away. I shook my head with dismay as Goodman strode up to the fireplace, casting his lamplight over Borley's shrine.

'Oh, Eric,' he chuckled. 'You sentimental old sod. You kept her flame burning all these years? You were a remedial fool as a kid and you'll remain that way until your last dying day.'

He placed the lamp on the hearth beside the candles and started leafing through Phyllis' exercise books, tossing them to one side as he shook his head. Rising, he placed the sack on to a desk nearby, peeling the hessian back as he removed a pick-axe from within, also from his office. I remembered now: his father was a miner – Goodman was always banging on about it in assemblies. Something else came out of the sack with the pick, fluttering to the floorboards. I could see the clippings by the moonlight, the red ribbon accompanying them as they hit the ground. Goodman bent and scooped them up, shoving them back into the bag.

I gasped at the sight of the old newspaper photographs and the telltale ribbon. It hadn't been the police who took the bundle of evidence. It had been Goodman!

'What is it?' whispered Dougie from his hiding place, having heard my startled exhalation.

Goodman stopped what he was doing, frozen like a statue.

'For pity's sake,' I said quietly to Dougie. 'Don't so much as breathe. I think he heard you.'

I watched on as the headmaster looked slowly over his shoulder around the room, lifting the lamp from the floor again to better search the shadows. Dougie, sure enough, remained motionless behind the fish tank cabinet, eyes closed in silent prayer. Slowly, Goodman put the lantern back on to the floor before stepping to the side of the fireplace, right beside Borley's shrine. Its glow illuminated his sweating face, eyes rolling, gripped by madness. He took the pickaxe and tapped the wall alongside the chimney breast, finally finding the hollow sound he was looking for. Stepping back, Goodman hefted the pick in the air and readied himself.

'I'm sorry I waited this long to come for you, Phyllis, my love,' he said, and swung the heavy iron pick at the wall.

With each impact of the weapon, Phyllis shuddered in my arms, as if the blows were physically hitting her. The tool was ripped clear after every strike, tearing away great sheets of plaster and splintered wooden slats. A cloud of grey powder was soon billowing around Goodman as he hacked and slashed the walls, scattering cement, bricks and rubble tumbling over the fireplace shrine. Spluttering and coughing, Goodman tossed the pickaxe back, the blade clattering into a desk and sending chairs toppling over. Wafting his hands vigorously, he cleared the air of dust, snatching at bricks and tugging them loose, throwing them back over his shoulder. I instinctively stood back, away from the missiles' flight, forgetting momentarily that they couldn't harm me. Phyllis looked up at me. Her hair was almost white now, her eyes red ringed, her lips blue. She was changing before my eyes, dying all over again.

'Help ... me ...' she mouthed, the words falling silent from her lips as the last crumbling brickwork came free beside the chimney breast.

I looked up as something fell from the wall cavity, Goodman standing to one side as it tumbled forward. It sounded like a bag of glockenspiel blocks, rattling and jangling as they struck one another. The misshapen bundle suddenly ceased its clattering descent, caught on the jagged bricks and plasterwork, hanging halfway out of the wall. The filthy pinafore was partially recognisable, as was the school tie around the neck, but it was the single red ribbon, caught up in a thin tangle of blonde hair, that caused my sudden intake of breath.

Goodman reached out, his fingertips fluttering over the dirty ribbon. He withdrew his hand, wiping it across his brow before turning to the sack. He opened it wide and laid it on the floor below where Phyllis' bones hung from the wall. It was at that moment that the rat that had startled Dougie in the corridor decided to strike again. Foolishly, it opted to attempt to share the fish-tank hiding place, but a hefty hoof from my best mate ensured that this rat was destined to almost go into space. It flew through the air and hit the wall opposite with a resounding squeak, before thumping to the floor.

With horror, I watched as Goodman turned back towards where Dougie was hiding. His eyes were wide and unblinking, reflecting the lamplight at his feet. There was a sheen of sweat across his bald head, mottled by masonry dust and plaster. He began to creep around the edge of the wall, picking up a brick as he drew nearer to Dougie.

'Mate, he's coming,' I hissed, willing my friend to move, but Dougie was frozen with fear.

'Don't be shy,' Goodman whispered. 'Out you come. It's you, isn't it, lad? Couldn't stay away, could you, Hancock?'

Dougie whimpered when he heard his name mentioned. He looked up as Goodman's lurching outline appeared through the murky glass of the fish tank, the lantern throwing his looming shadow across the ceiling above. His hand was raised, the brick poised to strike. My heart thundered as Goodman was almost upon my friend. Pushing Phyllis to one side, I found my fist aching, thrumming, ready to strike out at the headmaster. I needn't have bothered.

Putting his back into the cabinet, Dougie kicked hard against the wall, sending both cabinet and tank crashing down on to Goodman. The old teacher went down beneath a shower of splintering wood and glass, the contents of the tank spilling over him in a vile, stench-ridden wave. Dougie jumped up as Goodman roared, hurdling the broken cabinet and tank, slipping through the green slurry. He fell down in a heap, Goodman clawing at his legs. Dougie let loose a scream of pain as the man's hand raked his thigh, digging in and taking hold. Almost instantly the blood was seeping through his jeans, pooling in Goodman's liver-spotted hand.

'Hurts does it, Hancock?' he snarled from beneath the remains of the fish tank.

That was enough for Dougie. He kicked out, launching his free foot at the teacher's shiny head. Goodman's grip immediately loosened as Dougie rolled clear, crawling across the floor away from the stricken headmaster. Snatching up the pickaxe and staggering to his feet, Dougie turned back to Goodman, hopping unsteadily on one leg.

'Don't move, sir!' he said, the dusty tool held out in his trembling hands.

'I think we're past calling him "sir", mate,' I said, pulling Phyllis alongside me as we joined him.

'What do you intend to do, Hancock? You going to call the Old Bill, let them know you've caught me?'

'Why, sir? Why did you do it?'

'Enough respect, Dougie!' I said.

'Can't help it, mate,' he said, managing a flicker of a petri-fied smile for me. 'Old habits die hard.'

'What's that?' said Goodman, struggling to his knees, glancing in my direction. 'Are you still talking to yourself? Or is it the ghost of Underwood? You're sick in the head, boy.'

'Not as sick as you, you murdering swine!'

'Your friend Singer will live,' he sneered. 'He's an imbecile for wearing your grotty jacket in the first place. We've only delayed the inevitable. He'll be dead before twenty that one. I've seen it countless times. Moron has a death wish.'

'I'm not on about Stu,' said Dougie. 'I'm talking about Phyllis!'

Goodman glanced across to where Phyllis' bones still hung, partially removed from the wall cavity. 'It was an accident. She ... ignored me.'

'So you killed her and hid her body in the wall? That doesn't sound like an accident to me. And I don't think the rozzers will hear it that way eith—'

Dougie never got the last word out. The brick struck him across the temple, and he crashed heavily across the class-room. Stacked tables toppled and chairs collapsed around him as he fell to the floorboards, his forehead weeping blood. The pick was gone from his hands.

'Get up, Dougie,' I hissed. 'Please, mate! Get up!'

I was right down beside him, my lips to his ear, shouting at him, urging him back to his feet. He shook his head, trying to regain his balance and wits. The sound of something grating and scraping over wood made me turn, and Phyllis gasped. Goodman was on his feet, dragging his father's pickaxe across the classroom floor. He lifted it.

'Move!' I screamed, as Goodman brought the pick back. 'For God's sake move, Dougie!'

TWENTY-NINE

Cat and Mouse

The boards splintered where Dougie's head had been moments earlier, the pick buried deep into the rotten floor. My friend was already scrambling clear, crawling beneath tables and between chairs as he made for the exit, Goodman trying to worry the head of his weapon free from the timber. Dougie rolled and tumbled, kicking the furniture over as he hurried on his way, leaving an upturned obstacle course in his wake for the headmaster to navigate. I looked back as the pick was ripped loose, Goodman lashing out with his boots as he kicked desks and chairs aside.

'Crawl all you want, Hancock,' said Goodman. 'You won't be leaving the House, boy!'

He swung the pick like a battle-axe as he strode forward, shattering the furniture that blocked his way as he cut a path towards my friend. Dougie collapsed into the corridor, bouncing off the wall opposite.

'You have to get out of here,' sobbed Phyllis. 'Dougie! You must leave!'

'But what will he do to your remains?' he cried as he limped along, leaning against the wall. His right leg was no use to him. As always, the sensation passed across, my own limb now aching, shot through with a numbing pain.

'Does it matter?' she asked, as we heard the enraged headmaster approaching the doorway behind us. A darkness was descending over Phyllis. The black gloom that had infected her eyes upon our first meeting was beginning to return, but there was more to it than that. Her cheeks were hollowing, the plump bunches and red ribbons that had bounced when she laughed were fading now, losing what life they had. Her hair was thinning, just as on the disturbed corpse, and the ribbons were turning an ashen grey.

'I fear it does,' I said. 'Just look at yourself. He's killing you all over again! Where does your torment end? What will be left of you? You're our friend, Phyllis. We won't leave you!'

I bit my lip as Dougie kicked open a door, dragging Phyllis and me after him. Her dark eyes twinkled their last as she looked at me. Did I imagine tears there? Then they blinked out, hollow pools once again, the stuff of nightmares. The skin of her face and hands was stretched thin now, flaking and floating away as we followed our friend stumbling through interconnecting classrooms, trying to lose the crazed head teacher.

'Where are you, lad?' shouted Goodman, his demented voice echoing through the House's abandoned corridors and classrooms. 'Time for you to see the headmaster, Hancock. You've been a very naughty boy . . .'

His voice trailed off into a sickly chuckle which gradually disappeared. All I could hear was Dougie's frantic, laboured breathing as he worked his way from one room to the next, drawing ever nearer the landing. The occasional door slam or squeaking floorboard behind us told us that Goodman was nearby. I couldn't leave Phyllis alone. The condition she was in, strangled, choking, becoming a terrible shadow as her un-life faded: I couldn't abandon her.

'Think back, Phyllis,' I said. 'What happened that night? What did he do? That could be the key!'

'What's happened to Eric?' she whispered, her voice a strangled croak.

'Eric's fine,' I said. 'Don't worry about him. Look back into your own past, please. What did Goodman do? How did the accident occur?'

'Please, Will, don't make me look back there . . .'

'Trust me, Phyllis, please,' I begged her, squeezing her hands, brushing the thinning hair away from her skeletal face as it fluttered away like golden cobwebs on the breeze. 'The answer is in the past. Only you can do this.'

'I think ...' said Dougie, looking through the frosted glass of a doorway. 'I think that's the staircase. Perhaps I can make a run for it ...'

'What?' I said, turning my attention back to my friend and away from Phyllis. 'On one leg? He's probably waiting outside that door right now, ready to bury that pick in your back!'

'I can't wait here for the damn axe to fall,' he hissed. 'If I can get down the stairs, I might be able to get out of the window and start hollering. It's still early yet. If I can make it down the drive, someone's bound to hear. A commuter, anyone.'

'But can you make it that far?' I said, grabbing his arm with a ghostly hand, fearful emotions surging through me.

'I have to try,' he whispered.

I could have cried looking at Dougie's face. Blood was drying on his temple. One hand clutched his torn thigh while the other gripped the door handle. The iron knob rattled as the nerves coursed down his body and through his palm. I closed my hand over his, the shakes ceasing.

'I'll be by your side, mate. All the way.'

He nodded and yanked the door open. I peeked back as he set off in a stumbling run across the landing, but there was no sign of Phyllis. She had gone, disappeared into the darkness.

I cast my eyes about, searching the shadows for Goodman. Dougie hit the second-floor banister and began working his way along its length toward the staircase. He snorted through gritted teeth, each step clearly agony. I felt his pain as if it were my own, the discomfort shared between us. He was about to hit the top step when the pick lashed out from the darkness in the corridor, catching him by the ankle and bringing him down.

Dougie hit the landing with a thump, rolling over as Goodman's hands slipped around his throat. Again, I felt Dougie's pain, a stifling, choking sensation as Goodman squeezed the life out of us both. He struck my friend's head on the floor, Dougie's eyes bulging as he struggled in vain for breath.

She materialised behind Goodman, a smoky black form that coalesced in the gloom. As the shadows took shape, a pair of skeletal hands encircled the teacher's throat like a noose. She yanked her tormentor back, instantly tearing him free of Dougie. Her movement had knocked Goodman off balance, and he staggered into the banister on the landing. Dougie gasped for air, rolling on to his side as Phyllis' spectral form wavered in front of Goodman. *Now* the headmaster could see her. *Now* he saw his handiwork.

'It . . . it can't be,' he whispered from where he crouched on his knees. 'You're *dead.*'

'By your hand!' shouted Phyllis, her voice reed-thin and scratchy, like nails down a blackboard. 'Murderer!' A green aura shimmered about her wraith-like form, a dread wind blowing around her as she towered over the headmaster.

'You've got me all wrong,' he said, beginning to stand, one hand out, imploring, begging forgiveness. 'It was an accident!'

'Accident?' Phyllis gasped, her hand slipping around her own throat. 'You killed me. Strangled me with your own school tie. I didn't love you, but I didn't deserve to die . . .'

Dougie took a step toward the top of the staircase, the boards creaking beneath his feet. That was all it took. Goodman spun, the pick in his other hand rising high to strike him.

'Look out!' I screamed, alerting Dougie to the headmaster's intentions. My friend leaped forward, crashing into the teacher's middle and wrestling with him for the pick. The two of them collided with the banister, the wooden rail splintering as it gave way beneath their combined weight. I looked down, two lofty storeys to the ground far below. The sound of rending wood echoed through the House as rail, spindles and newel post were ripped free, and the struggling figures both tumbled into thin air. Towards their deaths.

'Leap!' I screamed, barging my friend free of Goodman's grasp and propelling him further out into space. Dougie collided with the great chandelier, its cobweb-covered crystals rattling as he was snared within its ornate arms and finials. The brass column lurched, grinding against its ceiling housing as Dougie's weight threatened to tear it free, but somehow it held, turning on its bracket and dislodging an avalanche of dust. I remained on the broken balcony, staring the short distance across to my friend where he was suspended, safe from harm. I peered over the edge, expecting to see Goodman far below.

The head of the pickaxe was embedded into the floorboards on the edge of the landing, while the shaft hung down over the landing's edge. Goodman hung from the end of it, both hands gripping the wood as his feet struggled for purchase against the wall. Digging the toes of his boots into the thin cracks of crumbling mortar, he looked across to Dougie with a grin.

'Well, boy,' he snarled, 'sitting pretty there, aren't you? Hang about and I'll be with you momentarily.'

With horror I watched Goodman raise one hand over the other, slowly hauling himself higher and walking up the wall. The axe head creaked where it was buried in the landing, the tool straining under the weight of the advancing headmaster. He grunted as he climbed, his eyes wild with murderous intent, his comb-over stuck to his sweat-slick bald head.

'Couldn't stay away, could you? Meddling little oik. Well, you like the ghosts so much, you can join them.'

The chandelier jingled as Dougie nervously shifted. He was a sitting duck. Once Goodman got back on to the landing, it would be the end for all of us. With Dougie gone, what would happen to me? We were joined at the hip, inseparable. Would he join me in limbo – or something worse?

Goodman's fingers scrabbled over the edge of the landing, their torn and bloodied tips struggling for purchase. I stared at the hand, a killer's hand. He needed to be stopped. Reaching forward I gripped the ring finger and focused, prising it loose. It pinged free, followed by the little finger as I looked over the ledge and glared down at Goodman.

'You're done hurting people,' I whispered as his terrified eyes finally focused on me. I don't know what it was that suddenly allowed him to see me. Perhaps having seen Phyllis, his mind was now open to the possibility of ghosts. The same had happened with Dougie, after all, once I'd first visited him.

'Underwood,' he burbled, spittle foaming on his lips. 'Think of what you're doing, lad!'

I hesitated, my hand wavering over his straining thumb, index and forefinger. Could I do it? Could I take someone's life? Would that make me any better than him? Before I could decide I felt a cold presence at my side, turning to find Phyllis had joined me. Her phantom black hand closed over mine, drawing it back.

'Let me do this,' she said. 'You shouldn't have to.'

'But you can't move things in the physical world, Phyllis, remember?' I said. 'It has to be me.'

'You've a good heart, Will. You couldn't take a man's life, no matter how evil.'

My shoulders sagged, the tears welling in my eyes as I looked across to Dougie. My friend stared back, a terrible understanding and realisation on his face.

I heard Goodman's low chuckle. 'Well isn't that a shame? One of you *can* harm me but won't, and the other *wants* to but can't. Stand aside, children. Let me show you how this is done.'

His other hand came up, seizing the head of the pick axe where it joined the shaft, Goodman's face rising above the landing's edge. The blade bit the board even deeper, twisting position with the sudden movement, the spongy timber crumpling around it. The sound of groaning wood made all three of us look back as the floor began to buckle, nails and screws uprooted as the ground began to lose its integrity. The gleeful look was washed off Goodman's face as he let go of the pick, the tool tearing free from the splintering timber flooring and tumbling into space behind him. It landed on the ground floor with an almighty *thunk*, embedded into the soiled lobby carpet, the other end of the axe head pointing skyward.

The floorboards were tearing free around Goodman now,

crumbling as he grabbed them and clattering from the landing. He slipped back with a screech, his sweaty hands snatching at the exposed joists, sliding ever closer to the drop, palms full of splinters.

'Help me,' he wheezed.

I threw my hands forward, ignoring my darker instincts. I snatched at his forearms as he continued to lose his grip, his fingers now leaving furrows in the disintegrating wood. I focused all my energy on Goodman's wrists, holding on tight, willing myself to halt his progress. Even Phyllis wrapped her arms about me trying to help. It was all in vain. Goodman tumbled back, his fists full of decayed timber, screaming as he cartwheeled backwards through the air. Dougie, Phyllis and I looked away, unable to watch the headmaster's descent. Goodman plummeted to the ground two floors below, his scream cut short as he landed on the pick in the centre of the lobby.

THIRTY

Goodbyes and Hellos

In the moments immediately after Goodman's death, the House, and all within, appeared to be in a state of shock. A deafening silence had fallen over the building, every noise muted as if heard underwater. Ghost though I was, my ears felt like they'd popped and my vision wavered. I was at ground zero in the aftermath of a bomb attack. I collapsed onto the top step of the staircase, holding my head in my hands as I tried to fix my gaze upon Dougie in the chandelier. Goodman's wasn't the first horrible death Red Brook House had witnessed, but we had to pray it was the last.

The aftershock lifted, the dust slowly settling across the stairwell and entrance hall, and the world returned to normal. Well, the normality that one expected when one was a ghost. The grating jangling of the chandelier brought me out of my daze as it swung suddenly, Dougie at the heart of it, looking to leap across to the staircase. More dust came down, followed by plaster, as the elaborate light fixture groaned under his weight.

'Stay put, Dougie, for God's sake!' I said as he dangled from the ceiling, surrounded by crystals and cobwebs. 'That thing could give at any moment.'

'You don't say?' he said sarcastically as the chandelier groaned.

'Are you hurt? You OK?'

'Never better,' he replied through gritted teeth. 'Would now be a good time to mention my vertigo?'

'I never knew you were scared of heights.'

'Neither did I until I ended up hanging on a rickety chandelier that might send me crashing to my death.'

I tried to smile, tried to laugh to show him I was with him, but it caught in my throat. After all the night's events, all I now wanted was to see him safe again. But what could I do? I couldn't run out of the door and fetch help. I couldn't open a window and shout for someone. I was tied to Dougie, already at my elastic limit, sat watching him, fearful of his ongoing predicament.

I glanced over the edge of the broken banister, turning away instantly when I saw Goodman's busted body far below. To my relief, I found Phyllis sat beside me, no more the blackened banshee from moments ago. She was her ghostly self once again, the torment lifted with the passing of Goodman. She rested her head on my shoulder and breathed a sigh of relief.

'It's over,' she whispered. 'It's gone. I could leave here now.'

'Do you want to?' I asked.

'The House has been my home for ages. I've roamed the corridors, stared out of its windows and sat in that classroom for longer than I care to remember. More than a home, it's been my prison. I don't . . . feel I need to stay here any longer.'

'This sounds an awful lot like a goodbye,' I said.

'It doesn't have to be. You could come with me.'

I smiled. 'I don't think I could do that. You've grown tired of your un-life. I get that: I understand it. If you'd have lived you'd be well into your sixties by now, like Goodman and Borley. Ghost I might be, but I'm also still a teenage boy. This is new to me. I died before my time, with so much more that I wanted to do in life. I'll never get the chance to achieve those things now, but who knows what I might be able to do in death? There are other ghosts in this world, all stuck here in limbo. Why are they here? What terrible thing has stopped them from moving on? There are mysteries that I can solve, I'm sure of it, just as we solved your mystery, Phyllis.'

'Just as you solved mine?' she smiled. 'You got the wrong bloke arrested!'

I laughed. 'Yeah, but we got the right guy in the end, didn't we? I can do some good. There's a life I can live even though I'm dead. I've an opportunity here, alongside that muppet over there,' I said, pointing to Dougie as my friend waved back.

Phyllis glanced back over her shoulder and I followed her gaze. At the end of the corridor a light shone from her classroom, bright and brilliant as it spilled out of the doorway.

We both stood, Phyllis straightening her pinafore. Sniffing back a tear she called across to Dougie. 'You look after him, you hear?'

I peeked past her down the corridor, toward the bright light. I wondered if I walked down there now and stepped through the doorway whether it would all be over in a blink of an eye . . . She squeezed my hand.

'Goodbye, Will Underwood,' she whispered, kissing me on the cheek. 'Don't let death hold you back. Go out there, my friend. Live.'

I reluctantly released her hand, our fingertips lingering until the last moment, as she turned and departed along the corridor. I turned away when I saw her reach the open doorway of her classroom, bathed in the warm, golden light. I closed my eyes as I heard the door close shut behind her.

*

We were alone until dawn. That was when the first squad car pulled up at the head of the drive to Red Brook House. They'd spied Goodman's car beside the open gates, left there by the headmaster the previous evening. Once Dougie's dad had reported his disappearance, the word had gone round the neighbourhood like wildfire, with every able man, woman and teenager searching for his whereabouts. A crowd had soon descended – including the local press – as the grim discovery of Goodman's body was the first thing to greet the police upon entering the House. The second was the teenage boy suspended from the ceiling two storeys overhead.

As if the town wasn't already aware that something big was happening at the House, by the time the fire engine drove by to extricate my friend from his chandelier, the grounds were teeming with life. By this time the police had already asked Dougie plenty of questions about what had happened that night. The discovery of Phyllis Carrington's remains, plus the ribbon and photos Goodman had brought with him, only confirmed my friend's account. Led out into the light with a blanket wrapped around him, Dougie looked every bit the survivor of a terrible ordeal, straight out of the headlines.

Mr Hancock was there, waiting for his son. The poor chap was distraught and looked older than ever, his eyes wet and bloodshot as he spied Dougie. I stood to one side, leaving the two to their reunion, son holding nothing back as his father enveloped him in his arms. When they finally parted, the flashbulbs began to go off as the photographers from regional rags tried to get their shot. I even spied a television news van pulling up behind the fire engine, their film crew trying to find their way through the crowd. The lady journalist who led the way seemed most dismayed when her own celebrity failed to part the mob.

'Looks like you're famous now,' I said to Dougie as his dad stepped up to talk to the police and press on his behalf.

'For fifteen minutes,' he muttered. 'It'll be a skateboarding parrot they're talking about next week, just you wait and see.'

'Dougie!'

Her voice was breathless as she burst through the line of police officers and fell into his arms.

'Lucy?' said Dougie, as amazed as I was to see her. She hugged him hard.

'We all thought you were dead, after what happened to Stu.'

'No, I'm ... I'm very much alive,' he replied as another volley of flashbulbs went off. He smiled nervously as one of the photographers asked the two of them to look his way.

I watched with befuddlement as Lucy whispered to Dougie.

'I'm so sorry I never listened to you before, when you came to me to talk about Will. I didn't take you seriously, what you were saying. I thought you were being cruel. If I said anything to upset you, I can only apologise. I just wanted to let you know, if you need someone to talk to, ever: I'm there for you.'

'You might want to call your attack dog off,' he mumbled. 'Vinnie Savage is quite protective of you, if you weren't aware.'

'I heard what you did to him on Danger Night, Dougie. It was very brave of you. Besides, you might just have put him in his place. He's gone into hiding since you punched him in the knackers.'

'Why come to me now, Lucy?' he said, aware of my close proximity. 'Why the sudden interest in me?'

'Will was a friend to both of us. If you genuinely think he's a ghost, I'm all ears.' She glanced over her shoulder at the cameras and crowds. 'And besides, you're a bit of a rock star now.'

Dougie frowned and looked at me. Dead and unbeating though my heart was, it broke a little more at that moment. I looked at Lucy on Dougie's arm and saw her for what she was. She might be attracted to some rum company (present gormless best mate excepted) but that didn't make her a bad girl. And yes, she was still by far the most beautiful girl I'd ever clapped eyes upon. The memory of cherry upon my lips would remind me for ever of what it meant to be alive. But I didn't know her, not truly. I'd been infatuated with her. She was fond of me – of that there was no doubt – we were friends and mischief makers. I had always been there for her, to listen to what she had to say, to go light-headed when she flirted. I had to ask myself though: did our friendship mean as much to her as it did to me? I'd never know. I'd never got to tell her how I felt, and I never would. I shivered as I thought of Goodman and his own obsession, how he'd allowed it to eat away at him, devour him and lead him on to terrible acts.

'Tell her you were lying,' I said with a heavy heart. Dougie arched an eyebrow my way. 'Tell her you were in mourning, that it was a passing madness. Tell her whatever you need to, mate, but don't let her think I'm a ghost.'

Once again, I stepped away from my friend, this time affording him some privacy as he spoke to the girl I'd loved. I couldn't hear the words, but I could see he was earnest, almost shamefaced as he tried to put her off the scent. Lucy frowned, shaking her head and looking about them. Did she believe him? Was she looking for me, even now after he'd denied my existence? Stop looking, Lucy: you won't find me. As the press clamoured to get Dougie's attention and his father fielded their questions, I stepped a touch further away from them, into the snow-banked shadows before Red Brook House.

Winter could no longer touch me – I was dead after all – but I'd never felt colder in my life.

THIRTY-ONE

Lives and Loves

After the drama at Red Brook House, the school had granted Dougie a leave of absence. This was time for my friend to convalesce, seek counselling from mental health experts, unload whatever demons were haunting his nightmares after his awful ordeal. Dougie had different ideas, though: here was an opportunity to kick back and have a holiday. His boxed set of *The Walking Dead* was duly hammered, the XBox took one hell of a beating, and he found himself strangely addicted to watching *The Jeremy Kyle Show*. The latter confirmed one thing: Dougie needed to get himself back to school, pronto.

It was the day before he was due to go back, and we'd been to the hospital to check in on Stu. He was recovering well, back to his old self, and the wheelchair they'd put him in was now his favourite toy. Stu insisted the other kids in the hospital – and certain members of staff – referred to him as Professor X. He'd even mooted the idea of shaving his head in true homage, although Dougie was quick to suggest from personal experience that this wasn't a good look. Doctors said Stu would be home by Christmas, although the nurses on the children's ward would've preferred him gone sooner.

We decided to walk home from the hospital, the day crisp, the weather clear and the snow crunching under Dougie's feet. The fur-trimmed hood of his parka had been stitched back on – badly – by his father, but my mate wouldn't have it any other way. We were in no hurry, the day was ours. We strolled past Brooklands High, our eyes lingering on the headmaster's office. Miss Roberts, the head of the sports department and the most senior teacher in school, had taken temporary charge as interim head teacher. It was she who had signed off on Dougie's sickness leave permission letter, admittedly begrudgingly. She was still convinced he wasn't right in the head. She was only half right.

We came to a halt outside the familiar iron gates, now with fresh chains and padlocks securing them shut. Red Brook House loomed in the distance, down at the end of the gravel drive, a fresh layer of snow sitting atop its crooked roof like icing on a cake. The tall dark windows looked like sightless eye sockets, its double doors a wailing mouth. It already seemed like a lifetime ago.

'They can't pull it down soon enough if you ask me,' said Dougie. 'The place is a graveyard. They should bury it underground.'

'Dunno about that,' I said. 'Forget Goodman and his wicked ways if you can. The House is a mausoleum, a monument to our friend.'

Dougie shrugged and nodded. 'Gone, but not forgotten.'

'Never forgotten,' I added.

'I thought you were gonna go that night you know,' he said. 'When that door lit up and Phyllis went on her way, I was sure you'd be with her.'

'And leave you behind?'

'Well I wasn't going to go with you.'

'Yeah, but you're my mate. I didn't want to leave you. And besides, I'd probably have never got through anyway. I bet there was some angel or security guard checking papers at the gate. Phyllis earned her chance to move on. We helped her solve the riddle of her death: she righted that wrong and saw justice done.'

'So, what? You're saying you've still got to tick that box before you can skedaddle?'

'Something like that,' I said. 'I'm not entirely sure, but I can only imagine that I'm stuck here until I discover who was driving that car.'

'But it could've been *anyone*,' Dougie exclaimed, scratching his head. 'It was a hit-and-run!'

'That isn't lost on me, and thanks for reminding me of what it was.'

'You might never find out who did it, Will.'

I nodded forlornly. Dougie was silent for a moment, chewing the thought over in his head.

'Hang about. If you never move on, does that mean you're hanging around me for ever or what?'

'Let's think about it for a moment,' I replied. 'Phyllis was tied to the House, unable to leave it. Ever. Why was that?'

'It's where she was murdered.'

'Spot on. So she was inextricably tied to that place, unable to leave it. The question is: why am I tied to you?'

'I ask myself that same question every day, usually a second or two after I wake up and find you staring down at me like some pug-ugly gargoyle at the foot of my bed.'

'Believe me, if I could be somewhere else, I probably would. Sitting in your room all night with only your snores for company isn't the greatest way to spend each night.'

'At least I leave the telly on for you.'

'Yeah, the Psychic Channel if I'm lucky!'

'I thought it'd be research for you? Y'know, swotting up on speaking with the dead and all that.'

'The people on the telly at three in the morning are no more psychic than Bloody Mary, I guarantee it.'

We both laughed, Dougie receiving an odd look from an old lady who was trundling by laden down with shopping bags. He was admittedly, to her eyes, talking and laughing to himself.

'You should be in school,' she grumbled. 'Blooming loony!'

'Ah the joys of being considered mad,' he sighed to me, his voice quieter now. 'You've a lot to answer for, Underwood.'

'Which brings me back to my point. I could've stayed at my folks' house after the funeral. When all this first happened,' I said, waving my hands up and down myself, aware that I was a ghostly apparition before his eyes. 'But I made straight for you. Why was that?'

'Ready access to the Psychic Channel,' answered Dougie with a grin.

'Seriously, though,' I went on. 'Of all the places I could've gone to, it was you I chose. I think I know why.'

'Go on,' he said.

'I spent so long thinking that my unfinished business was with Lucy Carpenter, chasing her around, trying to tell her my feelings through you. I was chasing a lost cause. It wasn't my feelings for Lucy that kept me tied to the world of the living. It was you, Dougie.'

'Sorry?' he said, a touch confused.

'Don't apologise, mate. I've stayed close to you, forgoing my family, because it's from you I get my strength. I can see it now.'

Dougie was quiet for a moment. I could see the hint of a smile and the colour in his cheeks as he soaked in what I was saying. His eyebrow arched suddenly, the teenage boy getting the better of him as he went to shove me away.

'You big bloody Jessie! So what do you do now, then?' he said, kicking snow at me and taking great pleasure in seeing it pass unhindered through my nether regions.

'Dunno. Solve ghostly mysteries, I reckon.'

'Like in Scooby-Doo?'

'You'd have to be Scrappy Doo of course,' I said, wagging my finger.

'Naturally,' he agreed. 'But what does this mean for *you*?'

'I guess I hang around, ad infinitum.'

'Ad infinitum?'

'It's Latin,' I replied.

'I know what it means! You're planning on being a pain in the arse to infinity and beyond?'

'Like a ghostly Buzz Lightyear, mate,' I said. 'You got a friend in me!'

'You'll get hacked off with it,' he said, wandering away, drawing me along after him via that invisible umbilical cord of friendship. 'I'm really not that interesting. Mark my words, you'll go out of your tiny mind with boredom.'

'Don't worry, Dougie, I'll be busy.'

'Busy doing what?' he said.

'Haunting you, buddy,' I said with a wink. 'Haunting you.'